JINGLE-BELL JAM

PAMELA M. KELLEY

PIPING PLOVER PRESS, INC.

CHAPTER 1

"Thank you for coming to see an old woman on such short notice." Jaclyn, an older woman who lived on the outskirts of the Rivers End Ranch property, smiled sweetly as she set a platter of cookies on the kitchen table. They were raspberry shortbread, dusted with powdered sugar and looked so good that they made Bryan Baker's mouth water.

"It was no trouble at all. To be honest, I've missed working on smaller projects like this. I really enjoy making furniture." Bryan was a builder and architect and his business had grown so much that he was doing more supervising and managing of big projects than actual carpentry work lately. So, he was happy to take on Jaclyn's kitchen job and build her a custom bookcase and shelving for her many cookbooks, pans and knick knacks.

"Good, that's settled then. Have a seat dear and help yourself to a few cookies. The fairies told me you have a weakness for raspberry jam. Do you take milk or sugar in your tea?"

"No, thank you." Bryan smiled. "I don't know who your fairies are, but I do like raspberry jam. These are delicious."

Jaclyn nodded. "The fairies are never wrong about these things. They tell me your turn is coming soon. Are you ready?"

Bryan really liked Jaclyn, but sometimes it was hard to keep up with her. He'd heard the rumors that she claimed to talk to fairies and gnomes and had so many pet rabbits that no one was sure of the exact number. There did seem to be a lot of them, that's for sure. He'd been greeted at the front door by a half dozen mostly white rabbits running around the front steps and there were two happily snoozing in the corner of the kitchen, curled up by the heating vent—the warmest spot. It was cold out, so maybe they were smarter than he gave them credit for.

"My turn for what?" he asked as he reached for a third cookie. They were very good.

Jaclyn took a sip of her tea, frowned and added a bit more sugar.

"Why for love of course! Unless you already have

a girlfriend? The fairies didn't seem to think that you did."

What an odd conversation. And how did these 'fairies' know his business anyway?

"No, no girlfriend." He sighed. "I've kind of given up on that. Or put it on the back-burner for a while. I've been focusing on work instead."

Jaclyn leaned forward and peered over her glasses as if she could see him better that way. "Now why would you give up? That's just silly. It's good to be a hard worker, but don't let life and love pass you by."

Bryan was quiet for a moment, not sure what to say. Finally, he tried to explain. "I really don't think it's in the cards for me. I did once, but, well that didn't work out."

Jaclyn tapped her fingers on the table and looked deep in thought. "You used to date Amy Carmichael I believe?"

Bryan still felt a wave of sadness at the mention of Amy's name. Their ending had been abrupt.

"Yes, we dated last year and I thought about asking her to marry me. But I never got the chance. She dumped me instead, and got engaged a month later, to her high school sweetheart. He was a star quarterback who went pro for a while. He moved back home and they reconnected." Bryan felt depressed just thinking about it and reached for

3

another cookie. Unlike him, Amy's fiancé, Troy, was in great shape.

"Troy doesn't have an ounce of fat on him. It's hard to compete with that," he said as he patted his stomach.

"You know," Jaclyn began thoughtfully. "I bet it had more to do with the connection they had and that shared history. She just wasn't the one for you."

Bryan nodded. "I know that now. But it stung at the time." Especially when Bryan looked in the mirror and compared himself to Troy. Bryan was a bit thick around the middle and admittedly had a hard time staying away from sweets.

It had never been an issue until the past year or two, as he wasn't as active as he used to be. He knew that he wasn't a bad looking guy, but his confidence had taken a hit when Amy dumped him. It was easier to lose himself in work than to put himself out there again and risk more rejection.

"Breakups are always hard. But the right person is out there for you and the fairies say it won't be long now. As long as you are open to it? Will you open your heart, Bryan and let love in?" Jaclyn looked at him intently and Bryan found himself nodding.

"Of course I'll be open to it." He grinned. "I can't wait to see who the fairies have lined up for me."

The next morning, Bryan spread a thick layer of raspberry jam on French toast that was already dripping with butter and dusted with powdered sugar. A generous drizzle of real maple syrup was the final touch before he took his first bite. When he looked up he saw two sets of eyes glaring at him. He took another bite and the staring continued, accompanied by two furiously twitching tails. Holly and Rudy, his Maine coon cats were mad that he wasn't sharing.

He sighed, then got two paper plates, and put a few tiny bites of French toast on each, making sure there was plenty of jam. They both liked the jam. He set the plates on the floor by their water bowls and they hopped down from the kitchen counter and began sniffing and licking their treats.

"Don't get too used to it," he muttered as he sat back down to finish his breakfast. Holly and Rudy ignored him now that they had what they wanted. He'd checked with his friends Jess and Jake who ran the vet clinic, when he brought them in a few weeks ago for their yearly shots. They agreed that as long as he didn't make it a regular thing, a bit of jam and bread wouldn't hurt them. They seemed as fond of the sweet treat as he was. He was on his last bite when his cell phone rang and he recognized Wade

Weston's phone number. Wade was the general manager of the River's End Ranch and also a good friend.

"Morning Wade, what's up?"

"Sorry to bother you Bryan, but I have a favor to ask if you're not too busy? I'm calling everyone I know that has a truck."

"Sure, what do you need?"

"The big truck that usually delivers the Christmas turkeys to the food pantry just died and is being towed to the shop as we speak. Maddie has one hundred turkeys at the market ready to be loaded into the truck. Could you pick up a few cases and bring them to the pantry? I'm on my way to get some and a few other guys are too, but we could use another truck."

"I can head over there now, no problem."

✳

Wade, and two of his brothers were already at the market when Bryan pulled into the lot. Several big young store workers from the meat department helped to load cases of frozen turkeys into all the vehicles. Everyone then unloaded them at the food pantry which was just a few miles down the road. They carried them into the walk-in refrigerator, filling it almost completely.

Wade's wife, Maddie was one of several volunteers that helped to run the pantry and she was there to oversee the delivery.

When Bryan set his last heavy case of turkeys down, he turned a little too quickly as he stood up and felt a sharp ping in his back. He slowly turned to stretch his muscles, but it was too late. He knew as soon as he'd felt the familiar shift that he was in trouble. It was the strangest feeling almost like a too-tight rubber band that when it released, sent a wave of stiff pain across his lower back.

He called his brother Clark when he got in the car and asked if he might be able to squeeze him in. Clark was a doctor with a focus in orthopedics and he'd treated Bryan the last time his back went out a few years ago. Clark told him to come right in. Fortunately, being a Friday, Bryan's morning wasn't as busy as usual so he could head into the office after he saw Clark.

Clark took some X-rays and reviewed his notes from the last time he injured his back.

"You have a slightly herniated disc. Could have been worse, you're lucky actually." Bryan wasn't feeling especially lucky. Clark gave him a referral to a physical therapist and then read him the riot act.

"The PT will help, but you need to make some major changes." Clark loved to joke around but he was very serious as he looked Bryan in the eye. "This is going to only get worse unless you lose some weight and start exercising to build up your core muscles. You should join a gym and get back into working out, do some strength-training."

Bryan sighed. He knew Clark was right.

"I haven't been to a gym in years, I'm not sure where to start, or how much weight I really need to lose," he admitted.

Clark looked him up and down. "You're not really that overweight, just enough that it's going to start causing you some issues if you don't get into shape. I'd like to see you lose fifteen to twenty pounds. Even ten pounds would be a step in the right direction."

Bryan nodded. "Okay, I'll try to do that."

Clark opened a desk drawer and rummaged through a stack of business cards before finding the one he was looking for. He handed it to Bryan. "Call Melanie. She's running the new health club at the ranch. She can hook you up. She's a personal trainer."

"I don't know about that," Bryan said. When he thought of people who worked with personal trainers, he pictured very fit athletic types, not someone like him. Besides, he remembered Melanie. She was Melissa's sister. Melissa recently married Jack, a local cop, and Melanie came with them to trivia when she visited a few months ago. Melanie was cute as could be. The thought of having someone that fit and pretty as his personal trainer was a little intimidating. Clark wasn't happy with his hesitation.

"Seriously, call her and make an appointment to go in a week from now. Your back should be feeling better by then and you can slowly start to fix those weak muscles. She'll walk you through everything and design a program for you. My buddy Charlie went to see her last week and said she is amazing."

Bryan tucked Melanie's business card in his wallet. "All right, I'll give her a call."

❄

"What do you think of this? For the month of December, with every spa gift certificate we sell, we include a month's free membership to the gym?" Melanie's boss, Wade Weston, paced around her office. It was their weekly meeting and as usual, Melanie was impressed by Wade's energy and creative ideas. It was what had sold her on the opportunity to move cross country and run the expanded fitness center. Like many resorts did, Wade wanted to open the fitness center to the public as a way to generate additional income for the ranch.

"That's a great idea. January is always a busy time for people joining gyms after the holidays and this will make it even easier. Will we do a general promotion to reach people who aren't receiving gift cards?"

Wade thought about that and continued pacing. "Yes, of course. We'll have to. Any ideas on how to structure it?"

"We could waive the enrollment fee if they join in January and offer a ten percent discount if they pay for the year up front. People like to save money."

"I like it! Let's do it."

Melanie made a note in her book, to get an email out as soon as possible announcing the holiday specials.

Wade stopped pacing and smiled. "Melanie, you're doing a great job. I'm so glad you decided to join us." It wasn't the first time he'd said that and it was nice to be appreciated.

"Thank you. I'm thrilled to be here, too." Melanie had been intrigued when Wade first mentioned the possibility of joining him at the ranch. But, she wasn't sure how serious he was until he'd reached out after she returned to Boston, and made her an official offer. She'd said yes immediately, put in her two weeks' notice and moved to Riston the following week.

It was hard to believe she'd been at the ranch now for almost three months. She'd been non-stop busy since she arrived, getting the new center ready for more members, and getting to know everyone at the ranch. Both she and Wade turned at the sound of a knock on the door and said "come in" at the same time. The door opened and Wade's wife, Maddie stepped inside.

"Is everything okay?" Wade said quickly and with a level of concern that surprised Melanie. Maddie was a masseuse and ran the spa that was in the same building as the fitness center. She and Maddie had bonded immediately and Melanie hoped to go to trivia with Maddie, Wade, her sister Melissa and the others who regularly played on Thursday nights at the ranch restaurant.

"I'm not feeling well. I'm going to head home. Jackie said she'd cover my last two sessions today." A look passed between the two of them and then Maddie glanced her way, "Must have been something I ate," she added.

"I hope you feel better," Melanie said. Maddie really did look as though she felt awful.

"I'll pick up Vivian and get some takeout for dinner," Wade said. Maddie cringed at the mention of food.

"I'll get some soup for you," he added. "I'll see you later at home." His eyes were full of concern as Maddie left and shut the door behind her.

"Maybe there's a bug going around," Melanie said as Wade started to pace again.

An odd look crossed Wade's face. "Could be," he said. "So, did you learn anything about how those MyTown reviews work?"

Melanie hesitated for a moment. Wade had asked her to look into something and he wasn't going to be happy with what she'd found out. "I did. Unfortunately anyone can open an account on the MyTown site and leave a review on any local business. They can say anything they want." In the past week, two one star reviews had popped up saying the Fitness Center at the ranch was overpriced and dirty. There were no other reviews posted yet so it really didn't look good.

"Is there anything we can do about it?" Wade asked.

Melanie sighed. "Social media can be a blessing or a curse. I do have an idea though. When I email our members telling them about the holiday specials we can include a link to the MyTown site and ask nicely that they leave a review to help us reach new potential members. Oh, and we could offer a referral bonus. Maybe they could win a free month of membership if someone they refer joins?"

"Both great ideas. Let's get it done." His cell phone dinged that he had a text message and he glanced at his phone and frowned. "I have to run. This was good though, I'll let you run with things."

A text message flashed across Melanie's phone as

well, as Wade left her office. It was from her sister, Melissa.

"Can you take a quick coffee break? I have some big news to share."

Melanie glanced at her schedule. She didn't have anyone else coming in for the rest of the day. She should be able to run out for a few minutes.

"I'll be at the store in five..." she texted back.

CHAPTER 2

"So what's your big news?" Melanie could tell that her twin sister, Melissa, was dying to share something with her.

"Shhhh, I'll tell you in a minute," Melissa said softly. They were in the book store that Melissa owned and operated, in the resort's old West town, which was a collection of shops and services that were popular with guests and local residents.

"Anna, we'll be right back. We're going to go grab coffees at Sadie's Saloon, do you want anything?"

"No, thanks. I just opened a diet coke. Have fun." Melissa's employee, Anna, turned her attention back to the register and a customer waiting to buy some books.

As soon as they got outside and started walking, Melanie took a deep breath of the crisp cool air and sighed. She hadn't lived in Riston long but oddly enough it had felt like home right away. She'd expected to be terribly homesick for Boston and was surprised that, while she thought of her former city fondly, especially Modern Pastry in the North End and their perfect cannolis, she didn't miss living there the way she'd expected to.

Boston was a lovely, historic city, but Riston had mountains and soaring green trees, sprawling ranches and horses. The scenery at times took her breath away. And she could feel snow coming soon. It was in the air, a telling, cool wetness that she recognized from living in Boston. She could tell when a storm was coming.

"Are you listening to me?" Melissa asked. Melanie realized she'd been lost in her thoughts and hadn't heard a word that her sister said.

"I'm sorry. I was spacing out for a minute, thinking about how beautiful it is here."

Melissa laughed. "That's right, you're still in the honeymoon phase. It was the same for me when I first moved here. I'm used to it now."

"So, tell me, what's your news?"

"I finished the book! And got a bite from a publisher!"

"That's fantastic! How did you manage that so fast if you just finished?" Melanie knew nothing about books or publishing. That was Melissa's world. In addition to operating the bookstore, Melissa wrote fiction too. Melanie was excited for her to realize her dream of publishing her first novel.

"Months ago, I sent a query letter and sample chapters to a few publishers. Most never bothered to reply but this one asked to see the whole thing, and now it's done."

"So, your timing could be perfect. Maybe they will fall in love with it and publish it!"

"Well, that's the other part of my big news. I've decided not to send it to them. I'm going to publish it myself! I've been researching it all while I've been writing this book and it seems like my best option. I'm excited about it."

"Wow. Are you sure you don't want to try the publisher first?"

Melissa laughed. "I'm sure. I ran the numbers and I think I'll do better doing it myself and it will be more fun. I get to choose my cover, pick the editors to work with, do it all."

"And with your business background I have no doubt you'll do great." Melanie pulled her sister in for a hug. "I'm so proud of you!"

"Thank you. So, enough about me. What's new with you?" Melissa asked as they walked into Sadie's Saloon and ordered their coffees. Sadie was busy with a line of customers so they didn't get to chat with her as much as they normally would. Once they got their coffees and started walking back, Melissa asked how she was liking living and working at the ranch.

"It's convenient for now as I'm spending a lot of time there, getting everything the way I want it. My cabin is cute. It's small but I don't need a lot of room right now, just a place to sleep. I have been thinking a lot though about where I go from here."

Melissa stopped walking. "What do you mean? You're not thinking about moving already? Leaving Riston?"

Melanie laughed. "No, of course not. I love living here. So much so that I'm ready to really put down some roots. I had the afternoon off yesterday and drove all around town exploring. I happened to discover a piece of land for sale, on a lake and it's just perfect."

"You're going to buy land? To build something?"

"Yes! I actually made an offer yesterday and they called this morning to tell me it was accepted. I used some of the money from my trust fund and it felt like the right thing to do. I want to build my dream house and settle down."

Melissa wrinkled her brow and looked hesitant. Melanie knew that she was just worried for her. Melissa was a worrier. "By yourself though? You don't want to wait until you get married first?"

Melanie smiled. "I used to think that's what I'd do. But, I'm tired of waiting. I don't need to get married to have my own house."

"No, I don't suppose that you do," Melissa agreed.

"You bought a house when you moved here," Melanie reminded her.

"That's true. But building one seems different. Bigger somehow."

"It is. And I'm super excited about it. I just need to find the right person to build it for me. Maybe Jack knows someone?" Melissa's husband, Jack, was a policeman in town.

Melissa thought for a minute. "I'll ask him. He should give us a few names for you to call. Jack knows everyone."

"Perfect. I definitely would like to talk to a few people before deciding."

⁕

*W*hen Melanie walked back into the health club, she noticed right away that Natalie, the front desk assistant, seemed a bit nervous. The club was quiet at the moment. It was mid-afternoon and Melanie knew that she didn't have any personal training sessions scheduled for the rest of the day. She'd been planning to catch up on some paperwork in her office.

"Anything happen while I was out?" She'd only been gone for maybe twenty minutes.

"I forgot to tell you earlier that someone called for you, to book a personal training session."

"Oh, that's great news. My calendar is pretty much wide open." Melanie laughed.

"Yes, well, I hope you don't mind but I saw that and he wanted to come in as soon as possible so I went ahead and booked him for today."

"Oh, that's fine. What time?"

"Now, actually."

The front door opened and a tall, handsome man walked in with an easy smile and big brown eyes. He was a little thick around the middle, but not overly so. And his face seemed familiar. He walked up to the front desk to check in.

"Hi, I'm Bryan Baker. I have an appointment with Melanie?"

"*H*i Bryan, I'm Melanie." She held out her hand, remembering that she'd met him when she went to trivia several months ago, before she moved to Riston. There had been a big group of them playing that night. Bryan looked nervous and uncomfortable and she wondered if he even remembered meeting her. He shook her hand and even though the contact was brief, she liked the feel of her hand in his. She smiled again and tried to put him at ease.

"Come on in, I'll show you around and then we can put a program together for you. I don't know if you remember, but we actually met a few months ago at trivia, when I came to visit my sister, Melissa."

"Of course I remember." He smiled, sending a spray of laughter lines dancing around his eyes and mouth. "How are she and Jack doing?" He seemed to relax slightly as she led him in and showed him around.

"They're good. Do you go to trivia often? I've been meaning to get there again, but I've been so busy since I got here." Now that the club was up and running though, and she'd hired more help, her own workload was easing to more normal hours. Melissa was always inviting her to join them for trivia and other nights out, and now she'd be able to start saying yes more often.

"I like to go. I don't get there as often as some of them do. It all depends on if my work is busy. But I go often enough."

When she finished showing him around Melanie ended the tour by the weights and they sat at a small table. She opened her notebook and prepared to take notes.

"So, what is your goal? That will help me to determine what kind of a program to set up for you."

Bryan thought for a moment. "Two things I suppose. I don't get enough exercise now that I have more employees and spend more time in front of a computer. I pulled my back out last week lifting something and it was suggested that I start working out, to help prevent this from happening again." Bryan smiled wryly and added, "My brother, Clark, is my doctor and he also thought it might be a good idea for me to lose a few pounds. Said that would help my back, too."

Melanie nodded. "Okay, I can work with that." She looked at him carefully and added, "I don't think you need to lose much. Once you start getting in shape you'll naturally lose some weight and start to make better, healthier choices."

Bryan grinned. "I hope so. I do have a bit of a sweet tooth. I've never met a cookie I can say no to," he admitted.

Melanie laughed. "I'm the same way. I'm not much of a cook, but I do love to bake."

"You'd never know it." Bryan smiled and Melanie realized she liked him. There was a warmth about Bryan and a humbleness that she found appealing.

"I pretty much eat what I want, but I make sure I spend some extra time working out if I go overboard. Sometimes you have to treat yourself though, you know?"

"I do."

For the next hour, Melanie worked with Bryan, showing him how to use the various weight machines and jotting down the different size weights he used and the number of reps on a file card so he could easily reference it the next time he came in if he wanted to work out by himself.

By the time they finished, Melanie had made her mind up about something else too. She had been planning to wait to hear back from Melissa once she'd talked to Jack about a few builders he would recommend, but now that she'd met Bryan, she knew who she wanted.

"What kind of building projects do you like to work on?" she asked.

"I'll do just about anything, remodeling an older house, large commercial construction projects, but my favorite jobs are custom residences. Helping someone to build their dream house, to see their vision come to life."

"Do you have room in your schedule for another project?"

"Sure. What is it?" He looked intrigued.

"I want you to design and build me a house! I just bought the land, a one-acre lot on Heron Lake."

"That's a beautiful area. I'd love to help you with

that. Let me know when you're ready to come to the office and we can discuss."

"Is next week too soon? Monday or Tuesday morning?"

He smiled. "Monday morning is fine. See you around ten?"

*B*ryan hummed happily to himself as he climbed into his truck and drove out of the gym parking lot. He'd been dreading his meeting with Melanie, especially as he hadn't been to a gym in ages. But she had made him feel so welcome and comfortable. For a split second he'd imagined asking her out to dinner, but then quickly dismissed the idea. Someone like Melanie would never date someone like him. He realized that she was just being friendly. Especially when another guy came over to ask her a question and she smiled sweetly at him too. She was just a nice, bubbly person and he'd do well to not read anything more into it. He did enjoy her company though.

He was also pleased that she was going to trust him to design and build her house. He wondered what she had in mind. The area she'd found was actually one he'd considered buying in at one time. He was so busy building houses for other people that he hadn't taken the time to build his own yet. His business had taken off faster than he'd expected. A steady and ever growing stream of referrals kept him busy. Eventually, he'd build his dream house. For now, he needed to focus on keeping his customers happy and the small house he bought years ago suited his needs just fine for the moment.

CHAPTER 3

a few days later, Melanie met her last client of the day at four. It was her second session with the tiny blonde woman and Melanie hoped that her first impression was wrong and that the woman had just been having a bad day the first time that she came in. She forced a smile as she reached the front desk to greet her.

"Hi Amy, it's nice to see you again."

The woman turned and her blonde ponytail whipped around. "I hope you'll go harder on me than you did last time. I have to lose two pounds this week." She didn't look like she had two extra pounds to spare. Amy had to be a double zero. But if she wanted a tough workout, Melanie was more than happy to give it to her.

"Be careful what you wish for," she said with a

laugh. They set off toward the weights and Melanie started her with a few stretches and then they got right into it. She upped her weights and repetitions and before long, Amy was panting and working up a sweat. Melanie kept her too busy to chit chat, which was a blessing as the conversation last time was mostly one-sided. Amy just wanted to talk about herself and how perfect her life was. She had a huge diamond ring and was engaged to a famous ex-football player.

Melanie didn't really follow football, so she didn't recognize the name and knew she wasn't as impressed as Amy had expected. Melanie was used to girls like Amy coming into the gyms she'd worked at over the years. They almost always had perfect makeup on while they worked out and there was a manic quality to them, a real fear of gaining weight and of being less than perfect. Melanie had never understood that. She worked out because she liked the way it felt and being healthy. Looking good was an added benefit.

When she finished her workout and was on her cool down stretches, Amy got chatty again.

"So, I about fell over the last time I came in. I ran into my ex, who was the last person I ever expected to see at a gym. He said he was seeing you for a session too."

That got Melanie's interest.

"Really? Who was that?" She couldn't picture any of her clients dating Amy.

"Bryan Baker."

Melanie was silent for a moment and realized her mouth was hanging open in shock. She closed it and quickly said, "Yes, he just started coming to see me. He's very sweet. I didn't realize the two of you knew each other."

Amy laughed. "I know right? He's probably the last person you'd expect to see with me. He is sweet. No one I would ever be with long term though, of course. Especially when Troy came back into town. Everyone says we look great together. Meant to be, you know?"

Melanie wondered what Bryan ever saw in Amy. He really should be thanking Troy.

"I'm sure. Maybe I should see about dating Bryan. Since he's single and all. I thought he seemed like a great guy." She said it without thinking, feeling oddly defensive on Bryan's behalf, but as she spoke, she realized that she meant every word.

Amy was speechless.

"You want to date Bryan? Seriously? You could probably date anyone in Riston—why him?" She seemed genuinely perplexed.

Melanie thought about all the reasons why. "Well, why not? He's about my age, has a good job, and a great smile. He seems really nice and thanks to you,

27

he's single." She smiled to soften the blunt edge of her words. But now Amy seemed irritated.

"Well, I don't think that's allowed is it? Isn't there some rule about not dating clients?"

"Oh, I don't know about that. I don't think so," Melanie said.

"There is actually, dear. It's not allowed. I made the rule myself." Melanie turned at the sound of a familiar voice behind her. It was Mrs. Weston, the founder of the resort. She liked the older woman, but she had an unnerving habit of turning up out of the blue, almost as if her radar had gone off and she sensed that her expertise was needed.

Melanie knew that Mr. and Mrs. Weston had officially deeded the ranch over to the kids, but Wade said that she sometimes had a hard time letting go and missed being involved in the day to day running of the ranch. So, every now and then, she dropped by, shared her wisdom and then flitted off again.

Melanie thought of Wade and Maddie and how that should have been off-limits too, yet now they were married. She realized it was probably wise not to bring that up. Instead she just nodded and smiled at Mrs. Weston. Amy seemed delighted for some reason that Melanie couldn't quite fathom.

"See, I knew it! Too bad, Melanie. Bryan is off-

28

limits. You'll have to find someone else to date." But then she added, "I'm sure that won't be hard for you."

Mrs. Weston looked more sympathetic. "I'm really sorry, honey. But I agree with Amy, I'm sure you'll have your pick of young men to date."

$\mathcal{B}$ryan was feeling pretty good the following Tuesday morning when he headed in for an early session with Melanie. He pulled into the lot at a quarter to eight and groaned when he saw Amy walking toward him. He never would have joined the gym at the ranch if he knew she was coming here. Last he remembered, she went to a gym downtown. She must have switched for some reason. She always did like to go to the newest places though. And he knew that she often worked out twice a day, often coming to the gym when they first opened.

"You're up early!" she said as she reached him.

"Morning, Amy. Just trying to get a workout in before heading into the office."

"I'm impressed. Are you still doing sessions with Melanie?"

"I am. She's reason I came here."

Amy looked surprised. "Oh, I thought maybe you

were just doing an intro session to learn how to use the machines. New people often do that."

He nodded. "I can see why some people do that. I like working with Melanie though. She's great." He smiled just thinking about her. He'd been in for several sessions now and was surprised to find himself actually looking forward to coming to the gym. A big part of it was to see Melanie. He liked talking to her and she made him feel like she was glad to see him too and that he belonged there. It was a good feeling.

Amy frowned and then spoke quickly, her words coming out in a rush, "It's against the rules you know for her to date any clients of the gym. Not saying you were going to but someone mentioned it the other day while I was here, so just thought I'd pass it on."

Bryan felt as though his good mood was a balloon and someone had just stuck a pin in it.

"Always good to see you, Amy. I should head inside," he said.

Amy smiled sweetly. "Have a good workout, Bryan."

*B*ryan glowered to himself as he put his gym bag in a locker and changed his shoes. He wondered, not for the first time, what he had ever seen in Amy. She was a very pretty girl and they did have fun, but she wasn't who he'd thought she was. He missed being in a relationship, but realized it might be a good idea to go much slower next time. To make sure he really knew the other person well. He knew he wanted to marry someday, but forever was a long time to be with the wrong person.

He thought it was interesting that Amy had warned him off trying to date Melanie. He could have told her it wasn't even something he was seriously thinking about. Of course the thought had crossed his mind. But, even if he'd wanted to do something about it, his own code of ethics wouldn't allow him to date a client. And since Melanie had hired him to be her builder, she was his client. Besides, he seriously doubted that he was Melanie's type anyway.

He pictured her with someone more like Troy. Or his brother Clark. Clark was tall, athletic and charming. And a doctor. Clark never had trouble getting a date, but hadn't been serious about anyone in a long time. Bryan could picture Melanie and Clark dating though. They'd make a good-looking couple. Maybe he should arrange for the two of them to meet. He was sure if they did, that they'd hit it off.

Melanie was waiting for him when he went out to the front desk. She looked him up and down and grinned. "You look thinner already. How many pounds have you lost?"

Bryan felt the tell-tale warmth of a blush spread across his cheeks. He was secretly thrilled that she'd noticed.

"Eight pounds," he said proudly. He'd been shocked when he weighed in at the end of his first week of working out and trying to eat better. It hadn't been as hard as he'd expected. He just ate a little less than usual and he found that he had more energy now that he was working out.

"That's a great first week! Well done." He followed her over to the weights area and she had an entirely different workout for him. They did a lot of the same things as before, but she mixed in different machines and free weights and he laughed when she had him try the balance balls. They were half moon shaped bouncy discs and it was hard to keep his balance and try to lift free weights at the same time.

"Go slow," she said. "If you feel wobbly, just stop for a minute or slow it down."

They chatted as they made the rounds and as usual, the hour flew by. Melanie was so easy to talk to and she made him laugh.

"So, my car stalled out this morning as I was coming down the hill and I panicked. I came this close to hitting a parked car. It was a good thing I remembered what to do at the last minute," she laughed.

"What did you do?" He felt like he should know the answer, but wasn't entirely sure.

"I put it into neutral and pumped the brake really hard. Then when it stopped, I just started the engine back up again and it was fine. I think it might be time to get a new car though, before the weather gets bad."

"That's a good idea. It could be dangerous if your car stalls out on snowy roads."

"Maybe I'll go car shopping this weekend. What do you drive?"

He laughed. "A big old truck. You need something smaller. What do you drive now?"

"A red BMW convertible. Not very practical for the mountains," she admitted.

He could picture her driving along with the top down, her ponytail dancing in the wind. "I bet it's a fun car though."

She grinned. "So fun. Maybe I'll hold onto it for a summer car and pick up something more practical for year round. Any suggestions?"

"My sister Cameron drives a Subaru SUV. She loves it. It has all-wheel drive and goes through anything."

"I'll keep that in mind."

When they finished up, after the cool down stretches, Bryan felt great and was glad he'd come in.

"So, I'll see you Friday morning?" He confirmed before he headed into the locker room to shower and change.

"Yes, see you on Friday. Oh, I think we're all going to trivia Thursday night. You should join us, if you're not too busy."

Bryan smiled as a thought occurred to him. "I'd love to and I'll see if my brother Clark wants to come. I think you met Clark?"

"The doctor? Yes, I remember him. We didn't get a chance to talk much though." She smiled. "See you Thursday!"

*B*ryan met his brother around noon for lunch at Kelsey's Kafe. They usually met up every other week or so there because they both loved Bob's cooking. Bob had a gift for comfort food and Bryan had a particular fondness for his fried chicken with gravy and mashed potatoes. He ordered it almost every time he went in. But not today, he was determined to keep making better choices.

"You want a salad?" Kelsi Clapper, formerly Kelsi Weston, stood behind the counter holding a pad of paper and pencil to take his order and she nearly dropped her pencil when he stated his order. Jaclyn and her good friend, Simon, were sitting a few stools down and they both leaned forward to see what the fuss was about. Clark was running a few minutes late, so he'd told Bryan to go ahead and order for him. Kelsi repeated his order, "Bob, did you hear that? Bryan wants a salad."

The kitchen door swung open and Bob walked out of the kitchen with his hands on his hips and walked over to Bryan.

"You seriously want salad? Why?" Bob looked dismayed at the thought.

Bryan shrugged. "Do I want a salad? No, of course not. I want my usual. But I'm getting salad. Trying to eat healthy. Doctor's orders." Bob seemed somewhat alarmed at the mention of a doctor.

"It's nothing serious. I just need to lose a little weight and get in shape. That's all," Bryan assured him.

Bob nodded. "Okay then. I'll hook you up with some salad."

He went back into the kitchen while Kelsi brought Bryan a glass of ice water with lemon, instead of his usual sugary soda.

"I'm impressed," Simon said. "I should be

ordering salad too, but well, I'm not. Figure I made it this far, might as well enjoy the rest of the ride."

"Is this Melanie's influence perhaps?" Jaclyn asked with a smile. "The fairies tell me you've been seeing her often." She looked pleased with herself for some reason that Bryan couldn't figure. She was sweet though.

"Yes, I've been taking some personal training sessions with her at the new gym. She's a great teacher." He leaned forward to share his plan with her, thinking she'd appreciate his attempt at match-making. "I'm hoping to introduce her to my brother, Thursday night at trivia. I think they might hit it off. She invited me to join you all."

Jaclyn's jaw dropped and Simon looked at her in confusion.

"What is it dear?" He asked. "I've never seen you at a loss for words before. Are the fairies talking to you again?"

"No, the fairies are utterly speechless. As am I." Jaclyn shook her head and Bryan had the sense that he'd taken a wrong step somehow.

"Did you say that Melanie invited you to join us at trivia?" she asked slowly.

Bryan wondered if she was starting to forget things. He supposed that was normal at her age.

"Yes, she was nice enough to invite me to join you all. I'm looking forward to it. I know Clark will too. Hopefully he isn't busy. I haven't asked him yet."

"Yes, it would be a shame if he's busy." Jaclyn raised her eyebrows and then sighed. "Come Simon, we should be going. I have things to do." She shook her head and muttered to herself as she and Simon settled the bill.

They left just as Clark walked through the door. As soon as he sat down next to Bryan, Kelsi set their meals in front of them. A turkey sandwich with fries for Clark and chicken, mashed potatoes and gravy with a side salad for him. It smelled amazing, but it wasn't what Bryan had ordered. Clark glanced at his brother's lunch and laughed. "So much for healthy eating, huh? It does look good though, I'll give you that."

"I really did order a salad," Bryan said as Bob came out of the kitchen and walked over.

"He did order salad," Bob confirmed. "But neither one of us was happy about it. So, I made a healthier version of his favorite meal. That chicken is baked, not fried. The gravy is made with beef broth instead of fat, and the mashed potatoes have milk instead of heavy cream. I went heavy on the seasoning, so the flavor should still be good. And I did give you a salad too. Let me know what you think."

Bryan cut into the chicken, dipped it into the gravy and potatoes and took a bite.

"If this is what healthy tastes like, count me in! Thank you."

Bob looked pleased. "It was a fun challenge. Maybe I'll add some lighter options to the menu. People have been asking for them."

He went back into the kitchen and Clark looked apologetic. "Sorry I doubted you. You look good. Working out agrees with you."

"Thanks. I'm down a few pounds, and it's not so bad going to the gym. I've noticed that it seems to give me more energy."

Clark nodded. "It really does. Helps me sleep better too. How do you like Melanie? A few of the other docs have said their patients love working out with her."

"She's great. I really like her. I think you might too actually. She's single and really pretty too. Do you remember meeting her at trivia the last time we went?"

"Sure, vaguely. We didn't talk much. There was a big group playing that night."

"What are you doing this Thursday night? She invited us to go. You could talk to her then."

Clark set his fork down. "Are you trying to set me up? What about you? You're not interested in her? You said she invited you to go."

"It was a general you. Just friends going out. She's not interested in me like that. And even if I was, she's a client. She hired me to design and build a house for her, so it's not an option even if I was interested."

Clark hesitated. "I don't know. What about when you finish the house? You met her first."

"I really think you guys might hit it off. Trust me, you're more her type than I am."

"I don't know about that. I will go to trivia with you though. That's always a good time."

CHAPTER 4

"You hired him already? I have three names from Jack for you. Bryan was one of them, but I thought you were going to talk to all of them before deciding?" Melissa seemed irritated with Melanie's news that she'd hired Bryan after their first session together. But Melanie knew as usual, that her sister was just worried for her.

Even though they were twins, they were very different. Melissa was naturally reserved and cautious and Melanie had always been the more outgoing and spontaneous, impulsive one. She always went with her gut reaction and it rarely steered her wrong.

"I did, and I'm sorry I didn't tell you sooner. Please thank Jack for me," Melanie said as they walked into the restaurant Thursday night for trivia.

"You can tell him yourself. He'll be here as soon as his shift ends. He won't mind though. He likes Bryan." Melanie knew that her sister was already over her initial irritation. She just didn't like surprises.

"Jaclyn and Simon are already here," Melanie said as she spotted the older couple at a large round table, with a pitcher of root beer between them.

"They're always the first ones here," Melissa said with a smile as Jaclyn saw them and waved them over.

"Where's Jack?" Jaclyn asked as they reached the table.

"He'll be here shortly."

She nodded. "Good. We can save him this seat." She patted the chair next to her.

"Perfect," Melissa said as she sat next to the empty seat by Jaclyn and Melanie sat beside her. "Who else are we expecting?" Melissa asked.

"I think the usual suspects are all coming, according to Lily that is," Jaclyn said. "I ran into her at Sadie's Saloon this afternoon. Popped over for an ice cream and a coffee. She does make the best coffee."

"She does," Melanie agreed. "The caramel nut is my favorite flavor."

"I'm a hazelnut girl myself." Jaclyn smiled and looked deep in thought for a moment. "So, I believe it's Lily and Cody, Bernie and David and Wade and Maddie. Though Lily did say something about Maddie not feeling well this week so she wasn't sure about them."

"She went home sick the other day," Melanie said. "But she was in today and seemed much better, so I hope we'll see them." She had only seen Wade for a few seconds earlier in the day, when he stopped in to sign some checks. His office was in the main building, along with Bernie, his right hand assistant, and Lily, who handled events.

Melanie had been surprised by how many events took place at the ranch. There was always something going on. She was looking forward to the week before Christmas, when there was something fun happening just about every day. Melanie loved this time of year. She always wanted the wonder and joy of the Christmas season to last longer than it did.

"Here they come now," Jaclyn said, as Lily and Bernie and their spouses joined them and sat by Simon.

"You came to see me!" he teased them. The girls gave both him and Jaclyn hugs before they settled into their seats. Melanie smiled watching them. She had a soft spot for Simon. He had such a cheerful attitude that it was contagious. He was well into his seventies and had a thick head of snow white hair and rosy cheeks. He worked part-time in the golf shop and still played now and again. Not as much as he used to though.

He was one of Melanie's first clients at the gym. He had as he put it, a 'cranky' hip and she put him on a weight training program to help strengthen his muscles and ease the stiffness so he could play more without injuring himself.

"Is Wade coming?" Melanie asked the girls.

"He's on his way to get Maddie at the spa and then they'll be over."

"Oh, Bryan's here!" Jaclyn said happily as Bryan and his brother Clark walked over.

"I invited Bryan," Melanie said.

"Really? How wonderful." Jaclyn looked pleased at the news and Melanie quickly realized that she'd gotten the wrong idea. Not that she wouldn't mind if there was something between them, but there wasn't. Not yet anyway.

"I mentioned it to him the other day at the gym. He's been coming to me for personal training sessions."

"That's lovely dear. Bryan is doing a job for me you know. He's making some kitchen shelves and a hutch. He does wonderful work."

Melanie grinned. "That's good to hear. I just hired him too, to design and build me a house."

"Oh! Well, we're both lucky girls then, aren't we?" Jaclyn looked delighted as Bryan and Clark reached the table. But Melanie noticed her expression change when Bryan shifted his position and Clark sat in the empty seat next to Melanie. The look on Jaclyn's face mirrored the disappointment that Melanie felt too. She'd been looking forward to chatting more with Bryan. Though she supposed she'd still be able to do that.

Clark smiled and held out his hand. "I'm Bryan's brother, Clark. I think we met before but it was ages ago."

Melanie laughed as she shook his hand. "We did. Briefly. When I visited Melanie. That week flew by. But Riston made a great impression. I moved here soon after."

"Well, we're lucky to have you. Bryan has been raving about your training. He hasn't been to the gym this much in years."

"I'm glad to hear it. He's doing great."

They both looked up as Wade and Maddie arrived and took the last two seats at the table.

Clark's phone beeped and he glanced at the text message and frowned.

"My first surgery just got bumped to seven a.m. So, I'll be heading in earlier than usual."

"Bryan said you were a doctor. What is your specialty?" Melanie asked.

"Orthopedics. Tomorrow's surgery is a woman in her early fifties who missed a step on her back porch and fell onto her elbow and wrist. Both are badly broken. I'll have to rebuild her elbow, it's really a mess."

"Just from falling on her porch? That's scary."

Clark nodded in agreement. "She could have benefited from your personal sessions. Strength training strengthens the bones and muscles. The older we get, the more fragile our bones get."

"You two look so serious," Bryan teased them.

Clark laughed. "Sorry. I've been boring you with work talk. Let's change the subject. What have you been doing for fun since you moved to Riston?"

Melanie realized that she hadn't done much of anything fun. Not yet anyway.

"Well, I think I'm boring too. I've mostly just been working since I moved here. I've been so busy getting the new fitness center going to do much of anything else. But, we're at a good point now and I can ease back a little on my hours. So, I'll start exploring soon."

"I've been working her too hard," Wade said. "We are close to hiring a few more people and once they're on board, I think Melanie deserves a few days off."

"Thank you, but that's not necessary," Melanie

said. She'd expected to work long hours when she accepted the position.

Wade grinned. "I think it is! Now, a more important question. What's everyone drinking? First round is on me."

Everyone put their drink order in. Melissa and Melanie both ordered chardonnay and Melissa ordered a draft beer for Jack as she knew he'd be arriving any minute. Clark and Bryan both ordered beer too. When their waitress, Barbie got to Maddie, there was a moment of silence and then Jaclyn pushed the pitcher of root beer her way and Maddie smiled. "That's perfect, I'll have root beer too." A look passed between Maddie and Wade and then between Bernie and Lily. Melanie sensed that there was something unspoken in the air. Maddie nodded at Wade and he squeezed her hand gently.

A moment later, Jack came rushing in and gave Jaclyn a hug before sitting next to her and Melissa. When Barbie returned with everyone's drinks, Wade waited until they were all delivered and then he raised his glass. "I have an announcement. Maddie and I are expecting."

Congratulations poured in and Lily laughed. "I knew something was up when you ordered the root beer."

"That gave it away for you too, if I remember?" Bernie said.

"It did. I crave that root beer now."

"Lily craves all kinds of things." Bernie laughed. She and Lily shared the office with Wade. "Every week, it's something new. This week it's pickle cupcakes."

Maddie looked horrified at the thought. "Do I dare ask what that is?"

"Exactly what it sounds like. Vanilla cupcakes with diced pickles in the batter and the whipped frosting. Sweet and savory. They're actually not bad," Bernie admitted.

"When are you due?" Lily asked Maddie.

"I'm just past three months now, so sometime in May. How many months is it now for you?"

Lily patted her stomach as she did the math. She hardly looked pregnant, but she usually wore free flowing clothes that hid her small bump.

"I'm almost six months. She is coming in early March."

The baby talk stopped as Arthur the trivia host came around with score sheets and asked their team name. They used a different one every week.

"Pickle Cupcakes sounds good to me," Bernie suggested.

"In honor of this evening's announcement, I approve of that name! Now please pass the root beer." Simon topped off his and Jaclyn's mug as Barbi came to take their dinner orders. Thursday night was buy one, get one, pizza night, so as usual, they ordered a bunch of pizzas and were almost done eating them when the trivia got underway.

Melanie noticed as she ate that the restaurant was very busy. Almost every table was full with lots of families, guests at the ranch as well as local residents who were regulars on Thursday nights. The bar was busy too as trivia drew a good crowd. There were eleven other teams playing, ranging in size from two people to a dozen or so.

It was a fun time, and a nice group of people and Melanie was happy to be there with them. She was a little disappointed though that she wasn't able to chat much with Bryan. He was deep in conversation with Wade. Clark was pleasant enough though and he certainly was handsome. He was taller and thinner than Bryan and had a sureness about him, a confidence, that Bryan lacked. Melanie noticed that several heads turned as different women walked in and saw Clark sitting with them. Their glances lingered a little longer on him than anyone else.

During the half-time break, Melanie noticed a pretty blonde woman at the bar who was keeping an eye on Clark. When he looked her way she smiled and waved and Clark stood a moment later.

"If you'll excuse me, I see someone from work. I'm going to go say hello."

Bryan turned her way after Clark left and asked, "Where did he go?"

Melanie nodded toward the bar, where Clark was already chatting with the pretty blonde. Bryan shook his head. "I thought that was over."

"Who is that?"

Bryan slid into Clark's seat. "That's Nancy, a nurse that he works with. I know they've dated some, but I didn't think he was still seeing her."

"She's pretty."

"She's okay. So, are you having fun?"

"Yes! And I'm so glad you came out too. Both of you," she added.

"Me too. I finished your preliminary design this afternoon. Do you want to come by tomorrow or Monday to go over it?"

Melanie thought for a moment. "We have an early session in the morning. If you want to bring your plans with you, we could go to Kelsey's Kafe and go over them at breakfast?" Bryan didn't say anything right away, so she quickly added, "Or Monday in your office is fine. Either way."

"Breakfast is great. I'm sure I'll work up an appetite. My trainer is tough!" he teased.

"Very funny!"

Clark returned to the table and Bryan went to move back to his seat and Clark quickly sat down.

"Stay where you are. I haven't had a chance to catch up with Wade in a while."

Melanie glanced around the table and saw Jaclyn smiling happily as she looked their way. Her expression mirrored how Melanie felt. Clark was friendly and she'd enjoyed talking to him, but handsome as he was, she wasn't at all attracted to him. It was his brother Bryan that she wanted to be close to. His hand brushed against hers as he reached for a napkin and she felt that curious tingle again. It was like he radiated a warmth that she craved and wanted to be near. When he smiled at her, she felt the strangest sense of contentment. She didn't understand it, but she knew she wanted more of it.

"Do you have any other siblings?" she asked.

"Just one, a sister, Cameron. She's the baby of the family."

"What does she do?"

"She's a nurse. She mostly works in the ER and the overnight shift because she's one of the newest on staff."

"Oh, that must be hard." Melanie couldn't imagine working those hours.

"She says it's not so bad. I'm with you though. I like a good night's sleep."

They shared a comfortable moment of silence before Bryan broke it by asking, "So, what do you think of Clark?"

The question took her by surprise. "He's very nice. Charming." That really was the word for Clark. He had an easy confidence that she knew many would find attractive.

"He is isn't he? He's single too," he added.

Melanie raised her eyes at that. "Are you sure about that? It looked like there was something with the woman at the bar, Nancy was it?"

"If there is, I doubt it's serious."

It almost seemed as if Bryan was trying to sell her on his brother. She decided to set him straight on that.

"I think Clark's a catch. But, he's not my type."

He looked surprised and something else flitted across his face that she couldn't quite read.

"No, what's your type then?" he asked.

Melanie smiled and looked him in the eye. "That's easy. I like nice guys, and I'm partial to dark hair, brown eyes and someone that is laid back and fun. I like hard workers and it's a bonus if they like to eat out. I like just about everything and I don't really cook, so…."

Bryan laughed, but it was a nervous laugh and Melanie worried that she'd surprised him by describing someone that was exactly like him. He'd obviously had no clue that she was interested.

He turned his attention back to the trivia game as a new question was announced and before she knew it, they were on the final question. Three teams were tied for first place so they bet all of their points to have the best chance at winning. The category was food, so both Melanie and Bryan felt pretty good about it. Until the final question was announced.

"Following her husband's death, Irma Rombauer penned this culinary classic in 1931."

Melanie glanced around the table and saw nothing but blank looks. Even Jaclyn looked stumped. Bryan shrugged. "I haven't a clue," he admitted.

"I really don't know either."

"The only thing I can think of is maybe the Fanny Farmer cookbook. That's easier to spell and remember," Jaclyn said.

"That sounds good to me," Simon agreed. "Unless someone has a better option?"

No one said anything, so Simon jotted down the answer and handed it to Arthur, who was coming around to collect them. He usually gave them several minutes to answer all questions except the final one.

"What do you think? Is it Fanny Farmer? That sounds good to me," Bryan asked her.

"I hope so. We might win if no one else gets it right."

"Or we will lose spectacularly," Jaclyn chimed in.

"Think positive," Simon chided her.

"I always do." Jaclyn patted his arm as Arthur prepared to announce the final answer.

"Irma Rombauer wrote…." He paused dramatically. "The Joy of Cooking! Congratulations to the Three Musketeers, our winners tonight."

"Well, that's that then. We'll see you all next week," Jaclyn said as she and Simon stood. They'd all settled the bill before the final question and Melanie remembered from the last time that everyone left as soon as trivia ended. It wasn't late, just a little before nine, but she found herself yawning and looking forward to climbing into bed.

She laughed when she saw Bryan yawning two seconds after she did. They both stood as well and she said, "Sorry, it's contagious."

"It's been a long day for me too. But I'm glad I came."

Clark leaned over and gave her a quick hug. "Great to see you again, Melanie."

"Thanks, you too."

She glanced at Bryan and after a second, he pulled her in for a hug too. It was far too brief for Melanie's liking though. She loved the way Bryan's arms felt around her. He was tall too, but a little shorter than his brother and it seemed to her, that they fit perfectly together. She wondered if Bryan liked to dance. She could imagine herself in his arms swaying to the music.

"What are you thinking about?" he asked softly. "You look miles away."

She smiled somewhat shyly. "Oh, nothing. Just tired I guess. I'll see you tomorrow morning, bright and early?"

"You will, and I'll bring the plans with me."

CHAPTER 5

Melanie took more care than usual with her hair and makeup the next morning before heading to the gym. She wore her favorite black Lululemon workout pants that were flattering without being too snug, and a baby blue long-sleeved t-shirt with the River's End Ranch logo on it. They dressed casually at the fitness center but she still wanted to look good, especially as Bryan was coming in for her first session of the day.

Natalie was already at the front desk when she arrived and greeted her warmly.

"Morning Melanie. Did you hear the forecast? They are saying snow flurries today." Natalie was a gem. She was a first time grandmother, in her early fifties and worked full-time mostly for something to do. She liked the social aspect of greeting everyone as they came in and the members loved her too. She remembered all of their names and asked about their families.

"No, I hadn't heard. I don't mind a little snow, as long as it doesn't collect too much." Fortunately, living at the ranch, she didn't have to drive often. But, she did need to step up her search for a new car and go shopping soon. Her BMW was terrible in bad weather.

"Oh, I added someone to your schedule. A potential new member is coming for a tour later this afternoon. Alison Reynolds."

"Thanks, Natalie." Showing people around the facilities was part of Melanie's job too, answering questions and getting them excited to join. She didn't have to do much though, as the fitness center sold itself. The equipment was mostly brand new and cutting edge and the locker rooms were lovely, and had both sauna and steam rooms.

One of the biggest benefits was that it was never too crowded. Unlike some of the bigger gyms, members never had to wait to use equipment or be shut out of a class because it was full. And the views couldn't be beat. Floor to ceiling windows looked out on the property and the mountains in the distance. It was a serene and inspiring view.

Bryan arrived right on time, and they got started right away. Melanie noticed that he was quieter in the morning. Most people were though, she found. Except for her.

"Natalie says it's going to snow later. I love watching it come down, but am nervous driving in it. I didn't have to drive much at all in Boston. Whenever the weather was bad, I kept my car in the garage and took public transportation. I really should go car shopping soon. I hate negotiating car prices though."

Bryan laughed. "I wish I had half your energy. You must be a morning person. Do you bounce out of bed wide awake?"

"Sort of," Melanie admitted. "I guess I am a morning person. I love getting up early and enjoying my coffee and the peace and quiet before the day gets underway."

"I'm the opposite. I was up for several hours reading after I got home last night and it was a struggle to get out of bed when the alarm went off this morning. But I'm glad that I'm here."

"I'm glad too, and you'll see it really does get your day off to a great start."

"You know, if you want someone to go to the car dealership with you, let me know. I got a pretty good deal on my truck not too long ago."

"Really? If you don't mind, I'd love that. I was thinking I'd go on Saturday as it's my day off."

Bryan smiled. "That works for me. We can go to

several places and make sure you find something you like."

After the workout, Bryan showered quickly, then Melanie followed him in her BMW to Kelsey's Kafe. It was already starting to flurry a little, but the Kafe wasn't far, so she wasn't worried.

Bryan waited until she parked and held the door open for her to walk inside. Melanie loved Kelsey's Kafe. It was such a cheery, warm place and the food was really good. Kelsi waved hello from behind the counter, where Jaclyn and Simon were holding court in their usual seats. They came in just about every morning, ate breakfast and then lingered over coffee, chatting with other customers that came and went. They stopped at the counter to say hello before heading to a table.

"Normally, we'd join you both," Melanie said. "But Bryan has some designs to show me, so we need a bit more room."

Jaclyn nodded in approval. "Bryan is designing you a house? I think that's just marvelous. Don't you agree, Simon?"

Simon had just taken a big bite of buttered toast. "Marvelous," he agreed once he could talk.

"Bryan, are you a sponsor again this year for the Jingle-Bell Jam?" Jaclyn asked.

"What is that?" Melanie hadn't heard anyone mention it.

"Yes, I am. I was surprised by how much business I saw from it last year."

Jaclyn turned her way and smiled. "It's a lovely charity event dear. A festival ball at the Founder's Hall just off Main Street. And it's for a good cause. I believe this year the food pantry was added to the list of local charities, the one that Maddie volunteers at."

"Oh, that does sound fun. Are you going?"

"Simon and I both are. We wouldn't miss it. You may want to check with Wade, maybe the fitness center could get a mention. I think the ranch is a big sponsor."

"They are," Bryan confirmed.

"Did you go last year, Bryan? I don't think I remember seeing you there," Jaclyn asked.

"No. I gave my ticket to Clark. That type of thing is more his style."

Jaclyn frowned. "Well, I hope you're going to go this year? Networking is much more effective if you are actually there! Not just a banner on the wall."

Bryan laughed. "I wasn't planning on it, but maybe I will."

A sly look flashed across Jaclyn's face. "They give you at least two tickets, right?"

Bryan nodded.

"Well, why don't you bring Melanie? It would be a fun night for you both."

Bryan hesitated and Melanie's heart leaped and then sank when he didn't jump on the idea. Maybe he didn't want to be stuck with her for the night.

"It wouldn't have to be a date. Melanie could go on behalf of the fitness center. I'm sure Wade would approve of that," Jaclyn said.

Bryan seemed to perk up at that suggestion. "I think that's a great idea actually. If you're interested, Melanie?"

If he only knew how interested. "I think it sounds like fun. I haven't had an occasion to dress up for anything since I moved here. And I love to dance. Will there be dancing?"

"They have several bands that will be playing, for an hour each," Jaclyn said. "They all volunteer their time. Everything from big band music to blues and even a little country. I think Lily and her brother's band might be there."

"That sounds so fun," Melanie said.

They said their goodbyes to Jaclyn and Simon and settled into one of the bigger booths. The restaurant was only about half-full so there were plenty of empty tables. Rachel, one of the newer waitresses, came over to offer them coffee and give them menus. As soon as she returned with their coffee, they put their orders in—an egg and cheese breakfast burrito for Melanie and scrambled eggs and a bowl of oatmeal and homemade applesauce for Bryan.

As soon as she took their menus out of the way, Bryan reached into his leather briefcase and pulled out the designs for Melanie's house. He unfolded a large sheet of paper and spread it on the table, holding it so that they could both easily see.

Melanie was impressed and excited as Bryan walked her through his design. It wasn't a large house, but it was plenty big enough and it was a nice mix of rustic wood and contemporary with high ceilings and soaring glass windows along the wall that faced the lake. An upstairs loft area could double as an office and was just off the master bedroom which had a gorgeous bathroom and French doors to a small deck where she could picture herself having her morning coffee and watching the sun rise over the water.

"There's no formal dining room, but the eat-in area off the kitchen is big enough to accommodate a larger group. The family/living room will have French doors out to an oversized deck and I know you don't cook much, but I still gave you a nice kitchen. In case that ever changes." Bryan grinned as he pointed out the roomy but efficient kitchen with its center island, and a stove that also faced the water, so Melanie could have a nice view as she cooked.

"Maybe I'll want to learn how to cook now that I'll have a view like that." She laughed.

Bryan went on to describe the other two bedrooms, and ended by showing a big basement.

"You could leave that unfinished and use it for storage or we could finish it and give you another room."

"What would you do?" Melanie hadn't even thought about a basement.

Bryan didn't hesitate. "I'd finish it. If it was my house that would be my man cave, with a big screen TV, a game table for playing cards, and soft leather sofas. That's me though."

Melanie could picture him lounging on the sofa, watching a movie or sports on a theater sized TV. It was a nice image. "Let's finish it. I'm not sure what I'll use it for but it will be nice to have it done."

"So what do you think?" Bryan asked when he finished going through all of the plans. "I can change anything."

Melanie smiled. "I don't want you to change a thing. It's perfect."

Rachel appeared with their meals and waited while Bryan moved the paper out of the way.

"I think you started here the same week I came to the ranch. How are you liking it so far?" Melanie asked Rachel as she set down their breakfasts.

"Oh, it's great. It's the perfect job for me right

now because the hours are so flexible from week to week and I need that if an audition comes up or rehearsals or something."

"Oh, what else do you do?" Rachel was a few years younger, maybe around twenty-three or twenty-four Melanie guessed. She almost looked like a model, very tall and unusually pretty, with long dark hair, fair skin and blue-gray eyes.

"I'm an actress," she said with a shy smile. "I know Riston isn't exactly the best place for that, but I've managed to do some local commercials here and there and some community theater. I'm not in a position to move because of family obligations, so I'm just trying to make the most of it and get some experience on my resume."

"You'll have to let us know when you're in a local show. I'd love to come and support you," Melanie said and Bryan nodded in agreement.

"Thank you so much! I really do appreciate that. Are your breakfasts ok? Is there anything else you need?"

"All set," Melanie and Bryan said at the same time and then laughed. Rachel scurried off to take another order and they turned their attention to their food.

When they finished, Bryan insisted on paying the bill. "It's a business meeting and you're the client."

"Okay then. Thank you." As they were walking

out the door she asked a question she probably should have asked earlier.

"When is the Jingle-Bell Jam?"

"Next Saturday."

"Oh, so soon. I'll have to go shopping for a new dress this weekend." When she'd moved cross-country she had totally cleaned out her closet, donating many bags of barely worn clothes to local shelters and thrift shops. She only kept clothes that she wore often and she couldn't remember the last time she'd worn a fancy cocktail dress. It would be fun to get something new and festive for the holidays. She was picturing a pretty red dress as she suddenly felt her foot slip out from under her. The snow was coming down quite a bit harder now and the temperature had dropped, making the ground below icy and slick.

"I've got you." She felt Bryan's strong arms catching her, lifting her back up until she was steady on her feet.

"Thank you."

He grinned. "I think you need to shop for more than a dress. What time is good for you tomorrow to go to the dealerships?"

"Anytime. Whenever it's convenient for you."

"Okay then, I'll be by around eleven."

❋

*W*ade popped into Melanie's office after lunch with good news.

"I just got last month's financial statement back from my accountant and the fitness center is doing great. We're way past where we forecasted we'd be. Almost double the number of new memberships to be exact. Thanks to you." Wade was quick to give credit, but Melanie knew it wasn't all due to her efforts.

"Thank you, but the marketing you've let us do, the referral promotions and the high quality is the reason. Once people see all that we have to offer, they are eager to join."

"We make a good team then!" Wade said and leaned back in his chair, looking quite pleased.

"Are you a sponsor for the Jingle-Bell Jam?" Melanie asked. "I saw Bryan this morning and thought you might be."

"You know, I did sign us up for that. With everything else going on around here, I forgot all about it. I'm not sure if Maddie is going to be up for going or not. She hasn't been feeling so great lately."

"With good reason." Melanie smiled. "Bryan has an extra ticket actually. So I could go with him and represent the fitness center—and then you and Maddie can still go if she feels up to it."

PAMELA M. KELLEY

"That's a great idea. You sure you don't mind going with Bryan?"

Melanie almost laughed. Men could be so clueless sometimes.

"No, I don't mind at all."

A few minutes after Wade left to head back to his office, Natalie called to let her know her next appointment had arrived. Melanie glanced at her schedule. It was Alison Reynolds, a potential new member. Melanie would give her a tour, answer any questions and most likely sign her up for a membership.

Alison was a petite woman in her mid-thirties with a sporty, blonde bob. She was new to the area too and was a stay at home mother with two small children.

"I love them dearly, but I need a break. You have child care here?" Was her first question as they walked around.

"We do. The Kid's Korral is on the premises, just outside the gym, so the children are close but not so close that you'll have to worry about them interrupting your workout."

"That sounds perfect."

Like everyone else, Alison was eager to sign up for a membership when they finished the tour. After she'd given Melanie a check for her first month, she mentioned that she'd just come from visiting another health club in town. It was a big national chain.

"They have a crazy special going on right now. But it's just not as nice there or as convenient. Their day care has limited hours. I actually feel a little bad for them. I heard that they've been losing members lately. Maybe people are coming here instead?"

"Oh. I hadn't heard that. I'm new in town too though. I'm so glad you've joined us. I know you'll love it here."

After Alison left, Melanie went back to her office and pulled up the MyTown site. With a sinking feeling she saw that two new reviews had been added for the fitness center. One was a raving five star review, mentioning the childcare, and the awesome classes. The other was a one star that was the worst one yet. The headline was "Scam", and the review was a strange rant, saying they'd been charged double and everything was awful. Melanie sighed and knew she'd need to address the bad reviews with Wade. As a new business, they couldn't afford to be losing potential new members.

CHAPTER 6

*B*ryan came by at eleven sharp the next morning. The air was cool and crisp with the familiar dampness that signaled more snow was on the way. The forecast was for several inches later that afternoon. Melanie knew she should have gone car shopping weeks ago, but better late than never she supposed.

She smiled when she saw Bryan. He was dressed for the weather in a bright red knit hat, red and black plaid fleece jacket and a puffy black vest over that. Melanie pulled a soft white wool hat on along with matching mittens and her warmest down jacket.

"Ready to go shopping?" Bryan asked.

"Almost." Melanie pulled on her snow boots and then she was ready to go.

"I talked to Melissa. She got a Subaru soon after she moved here and she said she loves it."

"Those are good cars. Not too expensive and you see a lot of them around here. We can go to that dealership first."

Twenty minutes later they were at the biggest car dealership in town and as they got out of Bryan's truck, the snow was starting to lightly drift down. It put her in a festive, holiday mood. She always loved this time of year.

They spent the next hour looking at various Subaru and Honda models and Melanie liked several of them, particularly a pretty, ice blue-gray Subaru Outback. She was tempted to buy it on the spot.

"Let's go to the other dealership first," Bryan said softly so that the salesperson couldn't hear him. "You'll get a better deal if you are a little less excited and willing to walk away."

"Oh, okay. I probably should investigate all my options anyway."

The salesman's face fell when they told him they were making the rounds and on their way to another dealership.

"Please do come back. I can talk to my manager while you're gone and am sure he'll make it worth your while if we can get a deal done today."

"We'll keep that in mind," Bryan said smoothly.

"You're good at this," Melanie said as they drove out of the parking lot.

"It's a bit of a game they play. I just went through it not too long ago."

Melanie looked at several Volvo and BMW SUV's, but she kept thinking about the less expensive Subaru in the unusual pretty pale shade. Bryan seemed to know by her expression as they roamed around the lot, that her mind was elsewhere.

"Are you ready to go back for your Subaru?" he asked with a grin as they climbed back into his truck.

"Yes!"

An hour later, Melanie had all the paperwork completed for the car she'd fallen in love with. The dealership needed to get it registered and process all the paperwork so she wouldn't be able to pick it up until the coming Tuesday, but then she would have a proper car for driving in the mountains of Idaho and could handle most bad weather that came her way.

"Are you hungry?" Bryan asked once they were back in his truck. "My mother dropped off a huge container of beef stew this morning. Want to join me for a bowl? My house is right around the corner. I can drop you off after we eat."

Melanie's stomach rumbled in response and she laughed. She'd lost all track of time and it was already nearly 1:30.

"That sounds wonderful, thank you."

A few minutes later, Bryan pulled into the driveway of a small, cottage style house. It looked cozy and had a nice farmer's porch out front.

When they went inside, there was a wood stove in the kitchen that was glowing merrily and two fluffy cats curled up beside it. They both stood up at the sound of the door opening and walked toward Bryan cautiously, keeping their distance from Melanie. They were gorgeous cats.

"This is Holly and Rudy, short for Rudolph of course."

"Christmas cats?" Melanie stood still and let them come to her. They sniffed slowly and then let her pet both of them.

"Rescue cats. My former next-door neighbors actually dropped them off on my porch in a cardboard box with a note to take them to a shelter. They couldn't be bothered to do it themselves before they moved away."

"And you couldn't take them to the shelter?" Melanie smiled, knowing Bryan was too much of a softie to give the cats away.

"No, I couldn't do it. I already knew them. They used to come visit whenever I'd sit on the front porch. I used to leave food out for them because they often seemed hungry."

"So, they adopted you first."

"Something like that. It was a week before Christmas when they showed up in the box and I never did know their names, so I picked out ones that seemed to fit."

"Can I do anything to help?" Melanie asked as Bryan got two bowls and a container of soup out of the refrigerator.

"Sure, if you want to pour some drinks for us. There's bottled water and diet soda. I'll have water. Glasses are in the cupboard by the sink."

Melanie poured two glasses of water and when the microwave timer dinged, Bryan brought the bowls of hot stew to the kitchen table and they sat down to eat.

"Your mom is a good cook." The stew was rich and flavorful with lots of tender meat and potatoes.

"She is. She told me that she's worried I might get too thin." He shook his head in amusement. "I told her I don't think she'll ever have to worry about that. I like food way too much."

Melanie smiled. "I do too."

When they finished, Bryan asked if she wanted a quick tour. "I haven't done much here, but I did finish the basement, so maybe it will give you an idea of what you can do with yours."

She followed him around, to the two bedrooms upstairs, which were both roomy and comfortable looking, the warm and welcoming kitchen, cozy living room and then downstairs to the basement, which was a lovely surprise.

"It's so nice!" Melanie exclaimed. She'd expected a dark room, but Bryan's basement had small, high windows that let in light and the walls were a creamy ivory shade that made the room seem bigger. There was a polished wood gaming table in the corner and two large leather sofas that formed an L shape facing a big screen TV. She flopped onto one of the sofas and sank into its softness. Bryan sprawled on the other one and picked up the remote.

"Do you have anywhere you need to be?" he asked. "I can run you home now or we could watch a movie and relax?"

Melanie stretched and pulled a fleece throw over her. She didn't feel like going back out into the cold just yet. Staying warm and cozy inside and watching a movie sounded good to her.

"I'm up for a movie."

Bryan scrolled through the Netflix offerings until he found a comedy that neither of them had seen. They spent the next two hours laughing and neither of them noticed that the wind and snow had picked up. By the time the movie finished it was after four and darker than usual for the time of day. They went upstairs and Bryan looked concerned when he opened the front door and saw blizzard conditions outside.

"It looks like it's getting bad out there. I should get you home." Melanie could hear the wind howling and was glad that she hadn't been out driving in her BMW. Bryan's truck was big and could go through almost anything. She was getting her boots on when there was a loud crack outside and a moment later the power went out.

There was only a few inches on the ground, but the winds were furious and the snow was coming down so hard that it was almost blinding. They got into the truck and the visibility was so bad that Bryan inched his way down the driveway and then suddenly hit the brakes hard.

"Sit tight for a minute, I'll be right back." He got out of the truck and walked to the end of the driveway. Through the swirling snow, Melanie could see him bend at the waist to look at something on the ground but the snow was too thick for her to see what it was. A few minutes later he climbed back in the truck and started backing it up.

"I'm afraid we're not going anywhere for a while. The winds took down a power line and there's a live wire across the driveway. There's no way to get around it. Hopefully the electric company will have guys out to fix it soon."

Melanie shivered, partly from the cold and also from the thought of accidentally driving over downed lines.

"We're lucky you happened to catch that," she said quietly.

Bryan turned the truck off and she followed him back inside. The cats gave them a quizzical look, surprised to see them again so soon.

"Feel like a hot chocolate? And another movie? You might be stuck here for a while. I am sorry. I had no idea it was going to get so bad this quickly. At least the generator works so we can cook, and watch TV. And we'll have plenty of heat from the wood stove."

"Hot chocolate sounds wonderful and I don't blame you at all. I didn't expect a storm like this. I thought we were just getting a few inches."

Bryan set a pot of water on the stove as his phone rang. He answered it and while he talked, Melanie guessed that it was his brother. He confirmed it was when he got off the phone.

"That was Clark. He was calling to warn me that the driving is terrible. There are downed trees and power lines everywhere. He's on his way to the hospital now, and said a PSA just came through on his phone from the police asking people to stay at home."

His phone dinged at the same time that Melanie's did. She looked down and saw the text message asking people to stay home for 24 hours for safety.

"Guess it's going to be a movie marathon," she

said as Bryan handed her a steaming mug of hot chocolate. They went back to the basement, watched another romantic comedy then took a dinner break and had more stew.

"I was thinking, if the power is out at the ranch, my cabin would be dark and cold. I feel lucky to be here for the storm."

Bryan smiled. "Well, I'm lucky too, then. I'm grateful for the company."

Melanie took a big bite of stew and realized getting stuck in the storm was a good opportunity to get to know Bryan better.

"Tell me about your family. I've met Clark. Is he the oldest?"

"He is. I'm in the middle, two years younger. And then Cameron. She's a year younger than me."

"And you said she's a nurse. Do she and your brother work together?"

"Sometimes, but not that often. She works in the ER, so she only sees my brother if he's called in to consult on a case. It happens though for unusually complex breaks. My brother's specialty is orthopedics."

"I've never broken a bone. I tried to break one once though," she admitted.

Bryan raised his eyebrows. "On purpose? Why?"

Melanie laughed. "It sounds crazy now, but when I was ten several kids in my class had broken arms or legs and I thought their casts with all the other kids signing it, were so cool. I didn't really want the pain of a broken bone, it was the cast I wanted."

"But you weren't successful?"

"No. I thought I had a great plan, too. I jumped out of a tree house and tried to land on my arm. But either I have strong bones or I wasn't up high enough. My mother read me the riot act so I didn't try it again."

Bryan laughed. "Well, I'm sorry you didn't get your cast. You didn't miss much, I can promise you that."

"You broke something?"

"Arm and a leg. I don't recommend either and the casts really aren't that cool."

"So, your sister is a nurse and your brother is a doctor. You never had any interest in going into medicine?"

"And my Dad is a retired doctor and my mother was a nurse. I'm the only one in the family not in the medical field. But I have passed out more than once at the sight of blood. When we were kids, my brother and sister loved that game Operation. I was always happier playing with my Legos and building stuff."

"So, you're doing what you're meant to do." Melanie noticed that Bryan's face lit up whenever he talked about building.

"It seems so. I can't imagine doing anything else. What about you? Did you always know you wanted to work in fitness?"

Melanie laughed. "No! My original plan was to be a ballerina. But as it turned out, I wasn't that good and I didn't want to put in the necessary time to get better. I kind of fell into it. I always used to love to go to the gym and I liked helping friends figure out what they needed to do to lose weight or get in shape. And then I realized I could get paid for doing it."

Bryan nodded. "Riston's very different from Boston I imagine? How are you liking it so far? Do you think you'll stay here?"

"It's so different. I love Boston, and I miss it, but I love it here too. When I came to visit Melissa, I had this overwhelming feeling that I could easily call this place home. When Wade mentioned he was looking to expand the fitness center and needed someone to run it for him, everything kind of fell into place."

"Sounds like it was meant to be. I'm glad you're liking it here."

When they finished eating, they put the TV in the living room on and Bryan added some more wood to the wood stove. It threw out a lot of heat and the kitchen and living room area was warm and cozy. Melanie knew if she'd been home in her cabin she would likely have been shivering in the dark. She wrapped a throw blanket around her as Bryan clicked through the channels. Storm coverage was on all the major stations so they watched that for a bit. It looked ugly out there. The winds were still strong and they were encouraging people to stay home until daylight when the roads should be clear.

While the news was on, Melanie took a good look around and liked what she saw. Bryan's house was friendly and warm, just like him. There were colorful watercolors and photographs of the mountains and outdoors on the walls. The colors were rich and masculine, shades of green, blue and gray. While she was gazing around the room, she felt something soft brush against the back of her neck and jumped a little.

"That's Rudy coming to say hello," Bryan said. Melanie noticed that Holly was pacing around on the sofa behind Bryan's head, with her tail twitching back and forth. After a minute she hopped down and started to knead his thigh while he scratched the back of her head. Rudy purred as he rubbed his head against her knee and then flopped on the sofa on his back, legs in the air. He looked up at her, his eyes pleading her to pet him, so she did. They were both very sweet. Melanie sighed. She was having a lovely night, relaxing with Bryan and his cats. She wouldn't mind doing this again soon. She shot a look at Bryan, admiring the line of his jaw with its hint of stubble. Being a Saturday, he looked as though he hadn't bothered to shave and it was a look she'd always found attractive.

He looked her way suddenly and smiled, surprising her. "Everything okay?"

"Yes! I was just thinking how nice and comfortable this is. I'm so glad you have a generator and that I'm not home freezing in my cabin."

Bryan laughed. "I'm glad you're here too and it is nice having a generator. That was a good investment."

"Do you have a busy week ahead of you?" Melanie wondered what else he did in his spare time and when she'd see him again. Hopefully for trivia on Thursday.

"Nothing too crazy I don't think. Though Wednesday night I'm venturing out to play ice hockey with Wade and Jack and a few others. They've been trying to get me to go for a while. I used to play a lot in high school."

"Oh, that sounds fun! And it's great exercise too."

"Yeah, that's what I was thinking. I haven't played in a long time though—I'm not in the best shape, compared to some of the others."

"You might be surprised actually. You've been doing weights for two weeks now. I was shocked one year when I only did weights in the winter, no cardio at all, yet when I went running it was like

I'd never stopped. The weights help your muscles to loosen up and build strength. I bet you'll do great."

Bryan looked encouraged. "That would be nice. I'm a little nervous, but I really am looking forward to it."

They watched a suspense movie and it was good but when it was almost over, Melanie couldn't stop yawning. Bryan looked over and saw her trying to hide it and yawned himself.

"I'm pretty beat. Do you want to stay up a while or are you ready to head up?"

"I'm ready." Melanie followed Bryan upstairs to his guest bedroom. It had a king-sized bed and a puffy yellow comforter. It was a cheery, comfortable room. Melanie turned to say good-night and almost bumped into Bryan. They were so close that she could feel that curious charge of electricity between them again. His eyes met hers and she found herself leaning toward him and closed her eyes. She opened them quickly when she sensed him move away and he cleared his throat. He was standing there holding an extra blanket.

"I grabbed this for you in case you get cold."

"Thanks." She took them from him and stepped into her room, shutting the door behind her. How silly of her. Clearly, they were not on the same wavelength. A moment later, there was a soft knock at the door. She opened it and Bryan held out a soft t-shirt and a pair of sweatpants.

"I thought you might want something to sleep in. My sister left these here over the summer and you are about the same size."

"Oh, great. Thank you. Good night, Bryan."

"See you in the morning."

CHAPTER 7

*B*ryan was up early the next morning. After feeding the cats, he took a walk outside to investigate and see if the power lines were still down. He was very glad to see that the lines were back up and power had been restored. He was sure Melanie would be eager to get home once she was up and had some coffee.

He made a pot of coffee and while it was brewing he pulled out a carton of eggs, some butter, bread and bacon. He still had a half a package of bacon from before he decided to eat healthier and he didn't want it to go to waste. A little bacon on a lazy Sunday seemed like a good idea.

Ten minutes later, he turned at the sound of footsteps on the stairs. Melanie walked into the kitchen looking sleepy and disoriented and very cute.

"Morning," he said. "Coffee?"

"I'd love some. Thank you."

He poured her a mug and while she was adding sugar and milk, he pulled the bacon out of the oven.

"I thought I smelled bacon. It looks amazing."

"Are you hungry? I just made breakfast."

"Sure. Can I help with anything?"

"No. Just have a seat. Everything is done." He plated up eggs, toast and bacon for both of them and brought everything to the kitchen table.

Melanie took a tentative bite of eggs and then smiled. "This is delicious."

He grinned. "You sound so surprised. I'm not much of a cook, but I can do eggs. Did you sleep okay?"

"I did, thanks." She glanced out the window. It was starting to snow again, just light flurries and it wasn't supposed to amount to much. But they didn't think it was going to do much yesterday either. He was sure she was eager to get home.

"We can head out to the ranch after we eat if you like. We're back on regular power now, and the lines have been repaired."

"Oh, that's good. I am curious to see how they fared at the ranch. Hopefully the power is back there if it went out too."

When they finished eating and both had a second cup of coffee, they headed out into the cold. Bryan would have been happy to hang out with Melanie all day. He'd been surprised by how much he'd enjoyed her company the day and night before. But he was sure she had plenty of other things she'd rather do other than spend more time with him on a Sunday.

The roads weren't too bad. The plows must have worked through the night clearing snow away and though they saw the occasional downed tree, there were no downed lines anywhere that they could see.

Bryan pulled up to Melanie's cabin and was relieved to see that her outside light was glowing. If her power had gone out at least it was back up now.

"Thanks so much, for everything," Melanie said. She grabbed hold of the door and then surprised him by asking, "Do you think you might go to trivia on Thursday?"

"I don't know. I hadn't really thought about it yet. Are you going to go?"

"I probably will. I had fun this week and I want to start getting out more and doing things in town. Now that I have some more time to myself."

"Well, maybe I'll see you there then. I should be able to go. If you like, I can give you a ride to the dealership on Tuesday, after our morning session. I'll be going right by on my way to the office."

"Oh, could you? I figured I'd probably just take a cab or see if Melissa is around but it's hard for her to leave the shop."

"I'd be happy to. I'll see you on Tuesday."

*B*ryan waited until Melanie was inside and then smiled to himself as he drove away. He was in a good mood and wasn't ready to go home yet. He called Clark to see what he was up to and he told him to swing by on his way home. Ten minutes later, he pulled into the condo complex where his brother lived and parked in the visitor spot just outside his townhouse. Unlike Bryan, Clark wasn't eager to be a homeowner. He worked long hours at the hospital and liked the convenience of condo living. He also lived closer to downtown and less than ten minutes from the hospital. It suited his needs perfectly.

Bryan knocked on the front door and Clark hollered for him to come in. Bryan stepped inside and smiled at the sight of his brother sitting at the kitchen table, the newspaper spread out in front of him, coffee by his side and his feet up on the chair next to him.

"You look comfortable."

"I am. Help yourself to some coffee."

"I've already had two cups, might as well have one more." Bryan poured a cup and joined his brother at the table.

"So, you had company last night? How did that go?"

"We had a nice time. Good thing Mom sent me home with all that beef stew."

"Are you going to see her again?"

Bryan could tell his brother had the wrong idea. "It's not like that. We're just friends. I'm giving her a lift to the dealership on Tuesday and I'll probably see her at trivia this week. You should go too, and talk to her more this time." Though Bryan had to admit, he hadn't been too disappointed when Melanie and Clark didn't seem to have a connection.

"She's a great girl, but she's not for me. That became obvious pretty quickly." Clark sounded amused.

"What do you mean?"

"You may not be ready to admit it, but you're crazy about her, and she seemed pretty into you too. You should ask her out, on real date."

"I'd love to," Bryan admitted. "But I can't."

"Why not?"

"Well it wouldn't be proper with her being a client and all. She's paying me to design a house for her."

"That's it? You could make that work somehow."

"It's not just that. I ran into Amy on my way into the gym. She happened to mention that Melanie's not allowed to date any members of the gym. There's a rule forbidding it."

Clark looked skeptical. "Amy told you this? I'd take anything she said with a grain of salt. See if there's any truth to it."

"I don't think I'm her type anyway. She's cute and in great shape. Honestly, I picture her with someone more like you or Troy."

"I think maybe you should give her more credit than that. I didn't talk to her long but she seemed smart and certainly nicer than Amy. I still say you should ask her out."

Bryan brightened. "Well, we are sort of going to the Jingle-Bell Jam event together."

"That fancy cocktail thing that I went to in your place last year?"

"That's the one."

"Well isn't that interesting. It may not be an official date, but you could make it an unofficial one. Put on a sharp suit and spin her around the dance floor a few times. Put those ball room dancing lessons we suffered through to good use."

Bryan laughed. "You know that has come in handy over the years."

"Sure has. I hated it at the time, but the ladies do appreciate a good dancer."

"All right. I'll just go and have fun and pretend it's a real date."

"Don't pretend. Make it real. Have a fantastic time."

The gym was quieter than usual on Monday. Everyone that came in talked about the big storm and how it had affected them. Melanie realized that some people had been without power for several days and for many, going to the gym was not high on their list of priorities at the moment. Natalie loved telling everyone that came in how excited she was that their new generator worked like a charm.

"I told Luke a year ago that I wanted a generator. He said it wasn't necessary but he finally gave in and was he ever happy when it kicked on electricity for us and he got to watch his college football shows."

Wade emailed to let her know he and Bernie would be by after lunch for their weekly meeting. Usually it was just Wade, but once a month, Bernie came too. As Wade's right hand assistant, it helped her to have a feel for all the different areas that he oversaw.

Melanie checked her schedule for the day and remembered that she'd booked a massage with Maddie at the end of the day. She tried to get in to see her once a month as a nice treat but also because it helped to keep her muscles loose. Maddie was great at breaking up and smoothing away any little knots of tension that built up during the month.

The morning flew and while she was eating a salad at her desk for lunch she thought to check the MyTown site to see if there was anything new there, good or bad. There were a few new good reviews, but unfortunately there were two new bad reviews, both one stars. One said the fitness center was dirty and the other said it was crazy expensive for what you got. Melanie sighed. She was going have to show these reviews to Wade. She printed out the bad reviews and made two copies, one for Wade and one for Bernie. Maybe they would have an idea for what, if anything, they could do about it.

At one thirty sharp, Wade and Bernie arrived and they took seats in Melanie's office across from her desk. Wade led the meeting and started things off by focusing on the positive.

"Good news, our weekly and monthly numbers are up. People seem to know about the fitness center now. I'm hearing lots of good buzz and the feedback from the resort guests is positive too."

"I overheard someone at the supermarket the other day talking about gyms and they said ours is much nicer than the big gym downtown," Bernie added

Wade frowned. "Idaho Fitness is one of the

biggest chains in the state. Their monthly member-ship fees are less than half what we charge and I just heard them advertising on the radio this weekend that they are doing a two for one end of the year special. When two friends sign up together, they both get the first month free. It's a clever deal."

"About Idaho Fitness." Melanie handed each of them the printout with the bad reviews on it. "I'm not sure if you check the MyTown site very often but we've been hit with a bunch of negative reviews. It's unusual enough that it made me wonder if they might be fake."

"You mean like fake news?" Bernie asked as she glanced at the reviews.

"Sort of. It's not unusual for retailers to some-times trash competitors in reviews like that."

"You mean put up a fake negative review to try to damage the competition?" Wade's tone was incredu-lous and had an edge of anger to it.

"Yes, exactly that. It's easy enough to do. People either do it themselves signing up for fake accounts or hire someone off Fiverr or other similar site to do the dirty work."

"Is there anything we can do about it? Other than sink to their level, which of course we won't do," Wade said.

"There's not much. The sites won't take anything

down unless you can prove that it was done maliciously."

"We'll have to think on this and come up with something. But in the meantime, let's focus on what we know we can do, which is just an amazing job for our customers."

"I did send an email out to the membership asking for reviews but we only got a few new ones," Melanie said. "Maybe we can take a different approach and send an email thanking our members for choosing us and asking for their feedback. We could also suggest that they leave us a review as it helps new members when they are looking to find out about a gym."

"I like that idea a lot. People like to be thanked, and they like to help. Bernie, can you help Melanie put something together for that?"

"Sure thing. I think that's a great idea too," she said.

"Maybe we can add enough new good reviews that it will bury the bad ones."

At a quarter to five, Melanie locked her office, said goodnight to Natalie and walked down the hallway to the spa for her session with Maddie. She loved going to the spa for treatments. It was a relaxing tranquil place and it was nice to be pampered and let all her worries and cares float away for the hour or so that she was there.

She helped herself to a cool cup of cucumber water while she waited in the tranquility room for Maddie to come get her. It was a beautiful room, with chaise lounges covered in white towels and pillows, and a fountain in the middle of the room that doubled as a foot soaking area. Melanie took her last refreshing sip of water as Maddie stepped into the room and walked over to her.

"Hi Melanie, so good to see you again. Are you ready to come in?" Maddie looked as pretty as always but Melanie thought she looked more tired than usual and wondered if she'd been sick or if it was just from being pregnant.

Melanie followed her into one of the treatment rooms. A gas fireplace glowed merrily in the corner while soft jazz music played in the background. Maddie stepped outside for a moment so Melanie could undress and slip under the covers on the massage bed. She laid down face first and settled her face into the soft donut shaped cradle that was just above the head of the table. The bed was heated and the warmth radiated through Melanie as she lay there. Maddie tapped lightly on the door and then came back into the room.

She kneaded the muscles on Melanie's back first.

That was always her tightest area and Melanie felt them relax as she worked on them.

"How are you feeling? Wade said you weren't feeling so great last week," Melanie asked.

"I'm ok. I thought it was a bug last week, but it may have been the pregnancy. I've been pretty sick this time. Fine one day and then miserable the next. It was different with Vivian. Of course that was over nine years ago."

"I don't know much about being pregnant, but I think I remember reading somewhere that it's usually worst in the first three months. So maybe it should be getting better?"

Maddie laughed. "You would think so, but I don't think this baby got the memo."

She placed her fingers Melanie's temples and made small circles, releasing tension as she went along. She worked her way down to her neck and spent time kneading where her neck met her shoulders. Melanie knew from her clients that both neck and back issues were common with people who sat at a desk working on a computer all day.

"It's really not so bad," Maddie said softly. "Wade is so excited. He doesn't even want to know what we're having until he or she is born. He thinks it will ruin the surprise."

"That sounds like Wade," Melanie agreed. "I'd want to know immediately myself. I figure it will be a surprise until that moment and then I'd get to go shopping!"

Maddie laughed. "I was the same way. Which is why I don't care so much this time around. It's fun seeing this happen through Wade's eyes."

"How does Vivian feel about it? Is she excited?" Melanie knew that sometimes children were not as excited as their parents, especially only children like Vivian.

"She is. I think she's old enough that she doesn't feel threatened like a younger child might. She likes the idea of being a big sister. Vivian's always been an easy child. She's happiest curled up with a book."

"That sounds like my sister, Melissa," Melanie said. "And now she writes stories and owns a book store. It's perfect for her."

"Everyone seems to find their place here at the ranch," Maddie said. Melanie thought about what she knew of Maddie's history, how she'd lost her husband unexpectedly and had been a single mother, struggling to make ends meet for a while until she built a new career for herself running the spa. And then of course, she and Wade fell in love.

"Wade tells me that you're very active at the local food pantry. How did you come to be involved there?"

"Well, I was a client first. Vivian and I went through a rough patch for a while after my husband died. We didn't have the best insurance. We didn't plan for him dying so young and there wasn't much money set aside for anything. Especially after the funeral bills were paid. It was because of Vivian that I pushed my pride aside and showed up at the food pantry one week to get some emergency staples. It helped me to get by until I could catch up. As soon as things turned around for me, I started to volunteer there as a way to pay it forward and give back."

"That's wonderful. I was thinking about getting involved with some charity work now that I'm more settled and have some free time. Do you need any more volunteers?"

Maddie laughed. "We'd love to have you. And we always need volunteers. There is a small team of us that runs the pantry. We divide the work up so it's manageable. It's just a few hours a month. There's a monthly delivery that comes in and everyone works one shift a month handing out food. And then of course there are the holiday food bags."

"Is that what the turkeys are for?" Melanie thought of Bryan and how the turkeys brought him into the gym.

"Yes, we put together bags for each family with a turkey and all the fixings. We do it at the church parish hall on Saturday morning. The bags are blessed at the Sunday service and then we hand them out that Monday and Tuesday night, the week before Christmas."

"What can I help with? I can do anything in the evening or weekends."

"The pantry is open Tuesday and Thursday afternoons and Saturday morning. We could give you a Saturday shift and we'd love your help assembling the baskets or giving them out, whatever you can do."

"I'll gladly do both, just tell me where and when."

"Oh great. It's really a fun time, putting all the baskets together. We have the church youth help too and order a bunch of pizzas. They look forward to it every year."

Melanie was looking forward to it too. When she lived in Boston, she'd often volunteered on Thanksgiving, handing out meals at a local shelter and she'd been hoping to find a way to get involved in Riston too, once she met people and learned what options were available to help.

"If you want to come in this Saturday, we could have you train with someone. Then you could stay and have some pizza and help us fill the baskets if you like."

"I'd love to. That sounds perfect."

Maddie finished up with her feet, and it was always Melanie's favorite part. Her feet often ached from standing sometimes for hours if she had back to back sessions and it felt wonderful to have someone knead them and release the tension. When Maddie finished and left the room so Melanie could change, she felt like she could easily close her eyes and drift off to sleep. She had to force herself to get up and get dressed. She knew she'd be in bed early. A cup of soup when she got home and then she would climb into her pajamas and curl up and watch TV in bed. She looked forward to it.

CHAPTER 8

*A*fter his session on Tuesday, Bryan gave Melanie a lift downtown to the dealership. It was a clear, sunny day though the air was cold and more snow was predicted. Melanie was eager to pick up her new car. She'd already put her convertible into storage for the winter. Melissa and Jack had an extra garage that they weren't using so it worked out perfectly. And Melissa had approved of the car she'd selected, which was the exact same as hers, just a different color. Hers was white.

Bryan was in an unusually good mood, Melissa noticed. He seemed to have more energy than usual and easily handled the extra weights she added to his routine this week.

"I'm down three more pounds, and sleeping better," he said as they drove into town. He was clean shaven this morning and she could see the difference in his face already. He looked great.

"That explains why you're in such a good mood. Congrats!"

As they pulled into the dealership lot, Melanie noticed a familiar figure with a blonde ponytail walking toward the big gym, Idaho Fitness, that was next door to the dealership.

"Isn't that your ex, Amy? She just recently joined our gym, wonder why she'd be going to this one too?"

"That is odd. Who knows why Amy does anything?" Bryan shook his head and didn't seem remotely interested as he parked and they got out of the car.

He left once Melanie was all set and the salesman handed her the key to her new car.

"I'll see you at trivia maybe later this week or at our session on Friday," he said as they walked outside together.

Melanie smiled. "If you go to trivia, I'll be there. Thanks for the ride."

She watched him drive off and a few minutes later, after familiarizing herself with all the car controls, she took her time driving out of the lot and heading back to the ranch. She loved the new car smell and it handled beautifully. She almost looked forward to the snow so she could try out the all-wheel drive. Almost.

Melanie still didn't plan to go far in snow conditions. She was terrified of hitting black ice and losing control. That had happened once before and even though she'd been driving slowly, she'd joined the fifteen or so cars ahead of her on the highway and slid all over the road until she came to a stop after sliding into a brand new Saab. It was an experience she wasn't eager to ever have again. But the all-wheel drive would be handy to get around town when she needed to.

When she got back into the office, Natalie let her know that the client for her next session had called to reschedule so she had some time to catch up on administrative tasks. Once those were done, she thought again about Amy and how odd it was for her to be going to another fitness center. She had never known anyone that belonged to two gyms before.

She pulled up Amy's membership to see when she joined. It turned out she was a very new member, and was there on a one month special offer Wade had advertised. It let new members join for a discount and try the gym out for a month. She'd only been in twice since she joined which was interesting, because one of those visits had been a personal training session with Melanie. She'd only been in one other time since, yet she had struck Melanie as someone who worked out often.

She looked her up on Facebook and then it made sense. Amy's fiancé Troy was a manager at the Idaho Fitness Center! Amy had likely joined as a spy to report back to him. Technically of course, there was nothing wrong with checking out the competition. But, it wouldn't surprise Melanie one bit to learn that Amy was behind the recent negative reviews on the MyTown site. At least some of them. The reviews were anonymous but Melanie pulled the site up again and took a closer look at the profiles of the reviewers that gave the one star reviews.

She wasn't surprised at all to see that all of them gave five star reviews to the Idaho Fitness Center and several also gave rave reviews to the upscale boutique on Main Street that Amy owned and ran. Now that Melanie knew this, was there anything she could do about it? That was the question. She guessed that it wasn't likely. The good news was that the number of positive reviews now more than outweighed the negative ones and new rave reviews were going up every day. But still, it bothered Melanie because it wasn't fair.

She was still trying to come up with a solution when her phone rang. It was Natalie saying there was a new member that wanted a session now and since Melanie was free, could she do it?

"Sure, I'll be right out. Who is it?"

"She says you know her. Jaclyn."

Melanie was thrilled. Jaclyn had mentioned she might come twice now, but she hadn't been sure if she was serious. She loved working with some of their older clients. She put them on light weight lifting routines that helped a lot with their flexibility and overall strength.

"I told you I'd come in," Jaclyn said when Melanie walked out to greet her. Jaclyn was wearing purple velour sweatpants and a matching jacket and had her hair pulled into a white bun with wispy tendrils escaping on both sides.

"You did. I'm so glad you made it in. Let's get started." Melanie gave her the usual tour and then showed her how to use some of the resistance machines and light free weights. They finished up with stretches.

"Okay, now can you take a little break? I brought us a post-workout snack," Jaclyn asked. "It's a new cookie recipe I need your opinion on."

"Sure. Can I get you a water or coffee to go with it?"

"I'd love a water, thanks. Meet you back here in a jiffy." Jaclyn went into the ladies locker room while Melanie poured two cups of water for them and sat at a small table near the front desk. Jaclyn joined her a moment later and pulled a plastic container out of an oversized tote bag that had rabbits embroidered on it. When she took the lid off, Melanie smelled sugar and raspberries. Lots of raspberries.

"I'm tweaking my raspberry thumbprint cookies. Usually I make a shortbread base. This time it's my usual snickerdoodles but with a dollop of raspberry jam in the center. What do you think?"

Melanie reached for one and took a nibble. Cinnamon and raspberry flavors danced and mingled together in a very delicious way.

"Yum. That's all I have to say." Melanie reached for a paper napkin to wipe crumbs from the corner of her mouth. Jaclyn looked pleased.

"Good. I thought it worked but I wanted to make sure. So, let's talk about what's really important." Jaclyn looked suddenly serious and Melanie leaned forward to pay close attention.

"What's that?"

"Tell me about Bryan."

Melanie smiled. So that's what was so serious? "Bryan Baker? He's doing great. He's lost more than ten pounds and has been coming in twice a week."

Jaclyn waved her hands in the air and made a face as she reached for another cookie. "I don't care about that. He looked fine to me."

Melanie laughed. "He did to me too. I guess I'm not sure what you're asking then?"

"The fairies are anxious for the two of you to

hurry up and figure things out. They have plans for the two of you."

"They do?" Melanie had heard about Jaclyn's fairies, but this was the first time she was aware that she was on their radar.

"You like him, right? Find him attractive, nice guy and all that?" Jaclyn seemed a little impatient that she had to explain what evidently should have been obvious.

"I do. I think he's great."

"So, what are you waiting for then? Make sure he knows so he can do something about it."

Melanie set her cookie down for a moment. "Well, there is a policy here that doesn't allow us to date clients. Mrs. Weston confirmed it."

"Hmmm, and who brought that to her attention?" Jaclyn asked.

"Actually, it was Amy, Bryan's ex."

Jaclyn raised her eyebrows. "And she mentioned that while Mrs. Weston was there? You do know that she's not actively involved in running the ranch any longer? It's been handed over to the kids. And if I'm not mistaken, Wade was a client of Maddie's as well as her boss. It doesn't get much stickier than that and they're married now."

Melanie laughed. "Well, that did cross my mind too. But I figured I'd not push my luck since I'm so new here. But I did think that I had shown interest. Maybe I'm not Bryan's type."

Jaclyn shook her head. "That's not it. Something else is going on. I'll get to the bottom of it. You'd make a good pair, the two of you." She peered over her glasses and added for emphasis, "The fairies are never wrong you know."

"Okay. Well if you talk to them, let them know I agree. We just need to work on Bryan."

Jaclyn stood and turned to leave. The nearly full container of cookies was still on the table.

"Don't forget your cookies," Melanie said.

"Keep them. Share with the others here. I have plenty more at home. Maybe I'll come back next week, maybe not. I'm going to play it by ear."

"Well, I'm glad you came in. Let me know anytime if you feel like coming in again. And thanks for the cookies."

❄

"I hit publish today!" Melissa said proudly when Melanie stopped into the bookstore on Thursday at the end of the day. They were going to walk over to the restaurant together for trivia night. It was just Melissa as Jack had picked up an extra shift and was working.

"You already got it edited, and published?"

Melanie was impressed. She followed Melissa out and waited while she locked the store door behind her. As they walked along, Melissa filled her in.

"I sent it off to an editor that was recommended. Eloise is awesome, and super fast. She read and edited the book in two days! I made all the corrections that she suggested, got the cover design back the next day and uploaded the book everywhere this morning. It just went live an hour ago!"

"How exciting! Send me the link when we get home and I'll be your first sale."

"Too late, someone already bought a copy. I have no idea how they discovered it, but I guess that is the magic of Amazon's computer algorithms. You can still buy a copy though!"

"I will. That's really great. I'm so proud of you." For as long as she could remember, Melissa had talked about wanting to write a book and now she had finally done it. And published it!

"I ordered ten copies of the print edition for the store too. Well, nine actually. Jack said he needs one and then we're going to frame it after he reads it. He wants to hang it on the wall."

"I bet that will look awesome."

When they arrived at the restaurant, everyone else was already there. Jaclyn and Simon, Bryan and Clark, Lily and Bernie, neither of their husbands were able to join them and Melanie was surprised to see that Wade and Maddie weren't there.

"Maddie wasn't feeling great again. Wade seemed worried when he left for the day," Bernie said.

"I saw Maddie earlier in the week for a massage, and she said this pregnancy has been a more difficult one for her," Melanie said as she sat down next to Bernie. Bryan was across the table, next to Jaclyn. Melanie was a little disappointed that she wasn't near enough to him to chat easily. But, she knew she'd be seeing him the next day for his session and then Saturday night for the Jingle-Bell Jam.

"I still need to get a dress for that," she murmured to herself.

Bernie laughed. "What was that? Are you talking to yourself?"

"I was! I just realized I'm running out of time to buy a dress for something I'm going to on Saturday. I'd almost forgotten I have nothing appropriate to wear."

"Oh, are you going to the Jingle-Bell Jam? We're both going, too. Well, Lily's band will be there and David and I are going with Jess and Jake."

"The veterinarians?" Melanie hadn't met them yet, but remembered Bryan had mentioned taking his cats in to see them.

"Yeah. Both Jess and Maddie volunteer with the food pantry which is one of the charities the event supports. I know Maddie and Wade were hoping to go, but it will depend on how Maddie is feeling."

"I hope she feels up to it. It sounds like it is going to be a lot of fun."

"It should be. I went last year and it's wonderful. Great food and music, a really good time."

About half-way through the evening, Melanie felt as if someone was looking her way and when she looked around she saw Amy and an extremely fit man with a crew cut sitting in the bar area. She guessed it must be her fiancé. Amy had a quizzical look on her face as she looked around the table. Her gaze narrowed when she saw Bryan laughing at something Jaclyn said. Bryan looked really cute when he smiled. Melanie noticed that, in addition to the laugh lines that she'd admired before, he also had a dimple in one cheek when he smiled really big. It gave him a playful look that was very attractive.

She couldn't help but notice that Amy didn't look like she was having an especially good time. She and her fiancé were barely speaking to each other and both kept checking their phones. That was a pet peeve of Melanie's. She hated when people stared at their phones instead of enjoying each other's company.

They did better this week at trivia and came in first place thanks to a final question about golf that only Simon knew the answer to. As they left, Melissa went to use the rest room and Melanie waited outside for her. Clark said goodbye as Bryan stopped to chat with her for a minute.

"I didn't get a chance to talk to you much tonight," he said.

"Jaclyn was glad to have you to herself. You two were thick as thieves." Melanie had noticed Jaclyn talking softly to him quite often throughout the night and wondered what they were gabbing about.

He grinned. "She fancies herself a match-maker I think. Her and the fairies."

At that moment, the door opened and Amy and her fiancé walked out. Amy did a double-take when she saw them.

"I didn't realize the two of you were here together." She looked at Melanie and raised her eyebrow, "Are you still working at the gym?"

Melanie laughed. "Yes. And we're not here 'together'—there was a big group of us playing trivia."

"How are you Amy? You look well," Bryan said pleasantly.

"I'm great thanks. Couldn't be better. Good night then."

Melanie watched her walk off and shook her head. "I can't figure her out."

"If I didn't know better, I'd say she's jealous. Which makes no sense because she dumped me,"

Bryan said. "I ran into her when I first came to the gym and she actually warned me not to even think about trying to date you. She said there's a rule against it or something."

"She did?" Melanie was horrified. "I'd say that's none of her business. Maybe she's regretting her decision. I noticed that she didn't look overly happy with that guy and you are looking better than ever."

Bryan looked surprised and pleased by the compliment.

"Thanks. I doubt it though." He spoke softly as he quickly added, "She is somewhat right about the no-dating rules. I have a similar policy with my work, not that it's ever been an issue, but I would never ask someone out if they were a client. It doesn't seem right. And I wouldn't want to get you in any trouble either."

That took Melanie by surprise. She wasn't sure what to say or think. Did it mean that Bryan would be interesting in dating her if not for the no-dating rules? Or not? She was relieved when she saw Melissa come through the door. "Right. Well, here's Melissa. I'll see you tomorrow morning for your workout."

CHAPTER 9

*M*elissa had a busy Friday. Bryan was her first client of the day and the conversation of the night before seemed to be forgotten. He was friendly and focused and said he'd see her the next night for the Jingle-Bell Jam. She had back-to-back sessions the rest of the day, ordered takeout Chinese for dinner and went to bed early.

She arrived at the food pantry at a few minutes before ten the next morning. Maddie was there to greet her and introduced her to Jess who was Wade's cousin.

"It's nice to meet you. A friend told me he brings his cats in to your clinic."

"Oh, who's that?" Jess asked.

"Bryan Baker. His cats are Holly and Rudy, Rudolph actually."

"Oh sure. The Maine Coon Cats. They're beautiful and very sweet. Maine Coons are friendly cats." Jess opened a box of canned tuna and restocked one of the shelves while Maddie put out the signup sheet for clients to sign in when they arrived. When she finished, she turned her attention to Melanie.

"So, let me show you around. We go shopping with the clients when they come in, and let them choose different items. The number of items depends on the size of their families, more food for more people. It's pretty straightforward. Dry goods are on the shelves, and then we have eggs and cheese and other dairy items in the refrigerator and frozen meats in the big freezer in the corner. The local bakery donates pastries and bread every week, so we let them pick that out for themselves as well."

Melanie followed Maddie around as the first few clients came in and then she started taking them around herself. There was a steady stream of customers for the next hour and a half. When the shift ended, she followed Maddie and Jess to the parish hall next door. The food pantry was built by the parish many years ago, and sat next to the main church.

"We brought all the supplies in here last night and now we'll set up an assembly line, putting each item that goes in the bags on a different table, so then the kids will just grab a bag and then go from table to table adding one of everything to their bags. We add the refrigerated items, butter, whipped cream and cheese, when the families come to pick up their bags next Monday and Tuesday night. And of course that's when they get a turkey too."

Melanie helped Maddie and Jess put all the food out on the tables. It didn't take long and Maddie explained that doing it this way saved a lot of time. They organized it with one item per table to help prevent mistakes.

"Once the bags are all made up, we'll have the kids bring them into the church so the pastor can bless them at tomorrow's service."

"How many do we make up?" Melanie asked. It seemed very well organized.

"We usually plan for a hundred but do an extra ten and they always go. People sign up ahead of time so we have a good idea of how many we need. There are always last minute additions though or people who think they signed up and aren't on the list."

"So, that's what the extras are for?" Melanie said.

"Yep. Every year we get a little more organized."

The parish doors opened and Wade and Bryan came in carrying five boxes of pizza each. A pretty petite blonde girl followed them carrying a bag of sodas and cups.

Melanie hadn't known that Bryan was coming to this. Though now that she thought about it, he had initially hurt himself by lifting the turkeys, so it shouldn't have surprised her that he was involved in putting the bags together too. Bryan smiled at the cute blonde girl and Melanie felt a pang of something. Who was she? She had never seen her before.

The doors opened and a dozen young children ran into the room followed by several sets of parents and a few minutes later another batch of children and parents. Maddie poured cups of soda while Jess set out paper plates and napkins.

"What can I do?" Melanie offered.

"Have some pizza." Maddie laughed. "We ordered extra this year to make sure we had plenty."

Melanie grabbed a slice of cheese pizza and then smiled as six adorable little Girl Scouts, dressed in their Daisy uniforms, walked in together and headed straight for the pizza.

"They're so cute!" Melanie said as she reached for a second slice.

"Aren't they?" Maddie agreed. "They come every year to help and they take it so seriously."

"Hi Melanie." Bryan walked over with the pretty blonde girl by his side. "I'd like you to meet my sister, Cameron."

"It's nice to meet you!" She was relieved to learn Cameron was his sister. Now that she took a closer look, Melanie could see the resemblance around the eyes. She had a kind smile as well.

"I've heard a lot about you," Cameron said warmly.

"All good, I hope," Melanie joked somewhat nervously.

Cameron laughed. "Yes. I hear you're going to the Jingle-Bell Jam tonight with Bryan. Clark can't make it this year, but I'll be there and my parents will be too."

Melanie looked at Bryan. "I didn't realize your parents were going?"

He nodded. "They go every year. My mother looks forward to getting all dressed up."

"I look forward to meeting them," Melanie said, but felt a bit intimidated at the thought of meeting his parents.

"They'll love you," Cameron assured her as she reached for another slice of pizza.

Melanie still needed to find a dress to wear and was planning to go shopping as soon as they finished up with putting the bags together.

"Did you eat?" she asked Bryan. She hadn't noticed him having any pizza yet.

"I had a turkey sandwich before I left the house. Trying to make better choices," Bryan said with a smile.

Melanie was impressed. "Smart. Now you can indulge a little tonight."

"Exactly. Oh, it looks like they are ready to begin."

Maddie called for everyone's attention and then Jess demonstrated how to fill the bags.

"I usually go around and slowly fill one bag and let the kids do the rest," Bryan said.

"That sounds like a good plan." Melanie did the same and watched with amusement as the little Daisies raced to fill as many bags as they could. They were fun to watch.

"See what I mean?" Maddie said as Melanie walked over to drop off her bag and a little Daisy ran in front of her to drop hers off first.

"They are very cute," Melanie agreed. She noticed a strange look flash across Maddie's face as she grabbed hold of the side of the counter to steady herself.

"Are you okay? What can I do to help?" Melanie asked.

"I think I just need to sit down for a minute." Maddie eased herself into a chair and ran a hand across her forehead. Melanie saw that it was glistening with sweat. Maddie didn't look well at all.

"Maybe Wade should take you home. We can finish up here. It looks like they are almost done."

Jess caught the tail end of what Melanie said and

looked concerned as well. "Melanie's right, Maddie. Go home and rest up. If you don't feel better, have Wade take you into the ER."

"Bryan and I rode here together. I could drive Maddie's car home, so she can ride with Wade. I don't think she should drive right now," Cameron added.

"I'll get Wade" Bryan returned seconds later with a visibly concerned Wade.

"Let's go," Wade said simply, allowing for no protest. He helped Maddie up gently and then walked her outside.

"I'll be by around seven to pick you up," Bryan said before he left with the others to get Maddie home and to pick up Cameron after she dropped Maddie's car off.

"I think Maddie pushed herself to come in today and it caught up to her," Jess said.

"I hope she's okay. She really looked exhausted."

"She did, didn't she?" Jess agreed.

"I can come on Monday and Tuesday to help too. You might need more help if Maddie isn't feeling well."

"That would be great, if you could make it," Jess said. Thirty minutes later, all the bags were done and in the church waiting to be blessed in the morning. Melanie helped Jess to clean up the pizza boxes and stray cups and then they locked up the parish for the night. Now Melanie had the rest of the afternoon to go dress shopping.

She drove to Lewiston, which was about an hour away and had more stores to choose from. Luck was with her as she found the perfect dress at Macy's, the first place she went.

It was a shimmery cranberry red cocktail dress with a scoop neck, long sleeves and a slim fit that flared out a little above her knees, giving it a flirty look. She found a matching pair of strappy high heels and a pretty string of fake pearls to complete the look. Satisfied with what she'd found, she paid for her purchases and drove back to the ranch with plenty of time to relax for a bit before she had to shower and get ready.

CHAPTER 10

Melanie took a deep breath as she ran a brush through her hair one last time. The dress fit her perfectly and she looked about as good as she possibly could, so why was she so nervous? And why did this non-date feel very much like a date? Was it just that she wanted it to be one? And wanted for Bryan to want that too? Or was it because she wasn't sure how he felt? Sometimes she thought she caught a hint of interest from him, when she'd catch him looking her way or holding her gaze a moment longer than normal.

But other times he seemed distant and he was so matter-of-fact the other night at trivia when he stated that he simply didn't date his clients, ever. But then she thought of what Jaclyn told her to do—to make sure he knew she was interested. Maybe that would make a difference? And if not, then she'd be a little embarrassed, but at least she would know.

A flash of light came through the window as she heard the sound of Bryan's truck driving toward the cabin. She added a final touch of rosy pink lipstick and was putting her long black coat on when there was a knock at the door. She opened it and Bryan stepped inside and took her breath away. It was snowing lightly and he was dusted with snowflakes but still looked so handsome in his crisp black suit and red silk tie with green embroidery on it. On closer look she saw that it was actually mistletoe all over his tie! That made her smile and gave her a little hope.

"You look nice!" she said at the same time he said, "You look beautiful." They both laughed.

"I love your tie."

Bryan grinned. "Thanks. Clark dropped it off yesterday, said he wore it last year and it was a hit."

"How's the driving?" Melanie glanced out the window and saw the snow starting to come down heavier.

"It's fine. This isn't supposed to amount to much, I don't think."

"That's what we thought for the other storm!"

"True. But I think this really is just going to be light flurries. Are you ready to go?"

"I'm ready." Melanie grabbed her purse and

gloves. She decided to skip wearing a hat because she didn't want it to flatten her hair too much. A few seconds later, she was in the truck and they were on their way.

It was a pretty drive into town, with the snow falling and the ground wearing a soft blanket of new snow. By the time they reached Main Street the snow had all but stopped as Bryan had predicted. The Founder's Hall was on a side street and as they drove about half way down Main Street, Melanie felt like a little kid taking in all the festive holiday lighting and decorations. There was even a giant Christmas tree that was all lit up and beautiful.

"They had the lighting ceremony for that last night. I had dinner with my parents afterward. It's kind of a family tradition for us."

"That sounds lovely." Melanie felt a moment of sadness, missing her own parents. She and Melissa had lost them to a car accident many years ago. It did get easier over time, but the holidays always brought occasional moments of sadness.

"I'll drop you at the entrance and then go park. It shouldn't take too long," Bryan said as he pulled the truck up to the front door.

"Are you sure? I don't mind walking with you."

He smiled, but insisted. "Go ahead, I'll meet you right inside."

Melanie walked into the lobby and the first

person she saw was Jaclyn standing near the door. She looked lovely in a royal purple sparkly dress, matching shoes and her hair was up and looked very white against the vivid purple.

"Well, don't you look lovely. Is Bryan parking?" Jaclyn asked.

"Yes, he insisted I come inside. You look very pretty yourself."

"Thank you. Simon did too. I think I'll keep him around. You should do the same!"

Melanie laughed. "I'd like to!"

A moment later, Bryan and Simon walked in together and Jaclyn said hello, then pulled Simon away to talk to someone they knew.

"Ready to head in?" Bryan asked. They checked their coats and then he led her into a large function room that was beautifully decorated with red, gold and silver. Bouquets of poinsettias were on all the tables, which were covered in crisp white linens. A tall tree sat in a corner, shimmering and glittering with gold and silver ornaments. Waiters wearing black with gold ties, circulated the room carrying silver platters of appetizers. There was a cocktail bar at either end of the room.

"Would you like something to drink?" Bryan asked.

"I'd love a glass of wine, a chardonnay please."

"I'll be right back." He went to the bar while

Melanie waited by a tall cocktail table and watched the crowd of people as they streamed into the room. She saw Jaclyn and Simon at the far end, chatting with a small group of people. In the center of the room a five-person band played soft jazz music, perfect for cocktail hour.

Bryan returned with her wine and a bottle of beer for himself.

"I ran into Bernie and David in line at the bar. They said they'd come find us."

"I was hoping that Melissa and Jack might come, but she said he's working." Melissa had said that they never bought tickets ahead of time for events like this because they never knew about his schedule.

"Clark was disappointed too that he wasn't able to come this year. One of his colleagues is on vacation and he is covering for him. He said it was a great time last year."

"It will be a great time this year too!" Bernie said as she and David joined them and set their drinks down and a waiter stopped by their table. They each took a bite sized spinach pie, which was delicious. "See, already great!" Bernie said with a laugh.

"I love your dress," Melanie said. Bernie was wearing a stunning, long black velvet dress that had a high neck and then dipped lower in the back.

"Thanks. I wore it last year too, but I'm hoping no one will remember."

"I told her she can make it her Jingle-Bell Jam dress and wear it every year, but that didn't go over so well," David said with a grin.

"I think that would be pushing it." Bernie laughed, and then waved as Jess and Jake walked in and looked around the room. Jess came over to the table while Jake went to the bar for cocktails. She looked pretty in a sleek navy blue cocktail dress. Her hair was twisted into an elegant updo. Both David and Jake looked handsome in their suits. David was wearing dark gray and Jake was in black. Both were wearing red Christmas ties. Jake's had cats and dogs in red Christmas hats which was perfect for a vet and David's had green Christmas trees. Melanie noticed, looking around the room, that most of the men were wearing creative Christmas ties, which added a fun feel to the event.

"I like that it's not too stuffy here," Jess said, echoing Melanie's thoughts. "We look forward to this every year."

Another waiter came by with skewers of marinated beef and they all took one. A few minutes later, it was scallops wrapped in bacon and then crab cakes and chicken on a stick with a spicy peanut sauce.

"I'm not going to want much for dinner," Melanie protested as the spinach pies came around again and this time, she said no.

"It looks like people are starting to sit for dinner. Should we get a table?" Jess suggested. They followed her to a round table that had room for all of them. Dinner was served soon after and it was an elegant meal of carved tenderloin with béarnaise sauce, roasted baby potatoes and sautéed spinach. There was a simple salad to start and freshly baked bread. Their server explained that there was a dessert table they could help themselves to and he brought coffee and tea for the table.

Conversation was lively during dinner and by the time they finished eating everyone was stuffed. But they still went to look at the dessert table and everyone found something to nibble on. Bryan picked a small pot of chocolate mousse topped with a raspberry sauce and whipped cream and Melanie was excited to see cannoli. She selected one that was dusted in sugar and the ends dipped in mini chocolate chips. They took them back to the table and Melanie sipped a cup of coffee while she savored the cannoli.

"What is that? I don't think I've seen one of those before."

"You love sweets and have never had a cannoli?" Melanie teased him.

"I usually go straight for anything chocolate," he admitted.

She broke off a piece of the cannoli and handed it

to him. "Try this. It's my favorite dessert in the world. Sweetened ricotta cheese in a crunchy cookie with a bit of chocolate on the ends. The best ones I've had are at Modern Pastry in the North End of Boston. But this is surprisingly good too."

"That is good. This is too. Do you want to try a bite?"

"No, I'm perfectly content with what I have. Thank you though."

"It looks like Lily is ready to play," Bernie said excitedly.

Melanie glanced over to where the jazz band had been playing. She hadn't even noticed that the live music had switched over to piped-in jazz. The five guys were gone and Lily, her brother Tyler and friend Marc took their places and a moment later the soft sound of a slow country music song filled the room.

They played several slower songs to transition from the quieter jazz but once it looked like everyone was done eating and starting to mill around the room again, they picked up the pace and played a more lively tune. It was the first time that Melanie had heard Lily sing and she was impressed.

"She really has a great voice," she said to Bernie. The song she was singing was one Melanie had recently heard on the radio. It was by a new artist and they were playing it constantly. She couldn't remember the name of the singer.

"You recognize the song?" Bernie asked and Melanie nodded. "Lily actually wrote that song and sold it to a music studio in Nashville. And now we hear someone else singing it all the time. I think it hit the top 10 on the charts last week."

"Wow. And Lily wrote it? Why doesn't she record her own music?" Melanie found that a little confusing. Lily's voice seemed good enough. Maybe not as memorable as the one on the radio but still really good.

Bernie smiled. "She doesn't want that. She's not interested in performing anywhere except locally like this. Her passion is the song-writing. Her best friend Laura lives in Nashville. They went to college together and I've heard her sing. Someday we will hear her on the radio, maybe even singing one of Lily's songs. How cool would that be?"

"Very," Melanie agreed.

"I want to dance," Bernie said and stood up. "David?"

He laughed and stood too. "Guess I've been summoned."

Jess and Jake made their way out to the dance floor too.

"Want to join them?" Bryan asked.

"I'd love to." They joined the others and they

danced five fast songs in a row and had a blast. When the music slowed Bryan took her hand and pulled her toward him and they swayed to the music. It was a lovely feeling, to be wrapped in his arms. She felt like she fit perfectly there and she didn't want the moment to end.

"Are you having fun?" Bryan asked softly.

"Yes. So much fun. Are you?"

"I am. I'm glad that we came."

"Me too."

"Have you spotted your parents and sister yet?" She hadn't noticed Cameron and was surprised.

"Cameron couldn't come after all. She was on call and got called in. My parents gave her ticket to one of their neighbors. They should be here somewhere. I think they came in a little late. We can take a walk around and see if we can find them. There's also a silent auction we can look at. There's usually some good things up for bid."

"Oh, I didn't realize there was a silent auction. I definitely want to take a look. Maybe I'll find something for the new house."

When the music slowed, instead of going back to the table, they visited the silent auction that was set up along the hall way. There were all kinds of items that had been donated by local businesses and residents, tickets to sporting games, gift certificates to local restaurants, various gift baskets, trips, and creative items like paintings. Melanie found herself drawn to a vivid watercolor that looked like it was of Heron Lake, where she was building her house.

"I love that," she breathed.

"It's very nice," Bryan agreed. "Put a bid in."

"I think I will." There were no bids yet, so Melanie picked up a pen and wrote a number in.

"Don't forget to check back later to see if you need to up your bid."

"There you are!" Melanie and Bryan turned at the sound of a woman's voice behind them.

"Hi Mom, Dad. This is Melanie."

"It's lovely to meet you dear. You work at the new fitness center at the ranch I believe?"

"I do."

"Pleasure to meet you." Bryan's father held out his hand and Melanie shook it. She could see the resemblance. Bryan's father had whiter hair but they shared the same eyes and he had his mother's smile. She was a petite woman with a smooth silver bob that fell cleanly to her chin. She had a very elegant style and was wearing a shimmery blue gray dress and a gorgeous diamond necklace and matching tennis bracelet.

"Come visit with us for a little while," his mother said.

"We won't steal you for too long. We know that you're here with your friends," his father said with a twinkle in his eye. Melanie like both of his parents. She could see where Bryan got his niceness from. They joined them at their table for a while and Melanie enjoyed chatting with both of his parents and getting to know them better. His father seemed to be enjoying his retirement and they both liked the theater and traveling.

"We're about to do the most marvelous trip that will combine both of our interests. We're going to fly to New York City for a long weekend and see a few Broadway shows and then we're going with a group on the Queen Elizabeth ship and crossing the ocean to London. There will be all kinds of theater and arts lectures on the ship and then we spend a few more days in London visiting various museums and attending more lectures and at night we will be seeing plays."

"That sounds like an amazing trip," Melanie said.

"We are looking forward to it. We've done other trips with this same group so we are looking forward to seeing some familiar faces when we go."

"Take lots of pictures," Bryan said.

His mother laughed and looked at Melanie. "He's teasing. We took so many pictures on our last trip that it was a little ridiculous. Bryan was a good sport though. He sat there and looked at all of them with us."

Bryan smiled. "I'm glad you had a good time. And

I do want to see plenty of pictures. I'm not kidding about that. It sounds like a great trip."

"Have you gone on that boat before and crossed the ocean?" Melanie asked. She pictured a grand ocean liner with fancy staterooms, sort of like the Titanic, but hopefully with more lifeboats.

"No, we're excited to though, and Harvey made sure they have plenty of lifeboats in case we hit an iceberg."

"Very funny," his father said and then added, "I did check though."

"I probably would too," Bryan admitted.

Big band music began to play and Bryan's parents turned to look.

"It's that band we like. Want to go for a spin?" Bryan's father held out his hand and his mother took it and they both stood.

"You two should go dance, too. Bryan is a very good ball room dancer," his mother said before they headed to the dance floor.

"You are?" Melanie asked Bryan. She hadn't expected that.

He smiled. "I'm not half bad I suppose. My mother made my brother and I take lessons years ago before some wedding we were in. It was a relative I barely knew."

"Well, you're probably much better than I am but I'm willing to give it a try if you are?" Melanie said.

"I'm happy to." Bryan took her hand and led her out to the dance floor. He put one hand on her waist and the other lightly on her shoulder and smoothly twirled her around the dance floor with an ease that surprised her. For such a big man, he was very quick on his feet and sure of himself. Melanie loved to dance and they stayed out there for three more songs before either of them was ready to take a break.

"Want to join the others?" Bryan asked as they came off the dance floor. Lily and Cody were there too.

"Did you get anything to eat earlier? I didn't see you guys until you started to play," Bernie asked.

"No. We ate at home and got here a little bit before we were scheduled to go on. My stomach is a little off these days and I'm not drinking. We're actually heading out in a few minutes."

"Lily's been really tired the past few weeks so we've been going to bed early."

"It is getting late. I don't think we're far behind you," Bernie said.

After Lily and Cody left, the band took a break and Bryan's parents stopped by to say they were leaving too.

"It was so nice to meet you both," Melanie told them.

"You too dear," his mother said.

"I hope we will see you again soon," his father added.

When the band came back for their second set, they all went to dance again. The first few songs were lively and Bryan whirled her around the dance floor until she was almost dizzy but she loved every minute of it. She liked it even more though when the music slowed and Bryan pulled her close to him. They played several slow songs in a row, to Melanie's delight. Bryan seemed to be holding her a little tighter than before and she liked it. She breathed in his scent, and sighed happily. The evening had been so much fun that she didn't want it to end.

But when they came off the dance floor she saw that the room was clearing out and the band was done playing. As they reached the table, everyone was standing and getting ready to leave.

"I guess it's that time already," Bryan said. He sounded as if he didn't want the night to end either.

"It flew by. But I suppose we have to go," Melanie agreed. They said their goodbyes to the others and got their coats from the coatcheck.

"Wait here. I'll go bring the car around. It should only take a minute."

Melanie watched through the front glass door until she saw the lights of his truck pull up. She climbed into the truck and stared at the lights along Main Street as they headed back to the ranch.

"Did you have fun?" Bryan asked as they drove along.

"I really did. It was a wonderful night."

"There are lots of other fun Christmas events coming up, most of them at the ranch."

"My sister told me about that. I'm looking forward to doing as many of them as possible. Cookie decorating and the Christmas Stroll and the hanging of the ornaments. I'll pass on the snowmobile racing though." She laughed at the thought of it.

"Well, you can cheer me on then. I almost won it last year."

"You did?" Melanie couldn't keep the surprise out of her voice.

Bryan laughed. "No, not even close. But I sure had fun."

"I told Maddie I'd help out Monday and Tuesday night after work handing out the Christmas bags. I think she's going to have me checking people in."

"I'll see you there then. I'll be one of the guys handing out the turkeys and helping some of the older folks carry their bags to their cars."

"I hope Maddie is feeling better by then," Melanie said, wondering how she was doing.

"I do too. We usually all go out that Tuesday

night after the last bag has been given out. It's sort of a tradition."

"You do? Where do you go?"

"There's a Mexican restaurant right on Main Street and we always go for margaritas and appetizers. They have great nachos."

"That does sound like fun," Melanie said.

A moment later she realized something. "I didn't remember to check back to see if I needed to up my bid on that painting."

"They'll call you if you won."

"Mine was the first bid. Somehow I doubt that it was the highest one," she said as Bryan pulled up to her cabin.

"You never know," he said as they both got out of the truck and he walked her inside.

"Thank you for driving and for tonight," Melanie said.

Bryan smiled and leaned toward her. Melanie held her breath for a moment and then released it when he dropped a sweet kiss on her forehead and then stepped back. She looked at him quizzically and then saw something in his eyes that gave her hope. She thought of Jaclyn urging her to make sure he knew she was interested. She took a deep breath and then stepped toward him and wrapped her arms around his neck.

"That was nice, but I think we can do better. You

are wearing mistletoe after all," she said softly as she leaned in and touched her lips to his. She felt him hesitate at first, as she took him by surprise but then he kissed her back and she melted into him for a long, sweet kiss. Finally they stopped and just looked at each other.

"Now, that was fun," Melanie said.

"It was, but..." Bryan began.

Melanie touched a finger to his lips and he smiled and was silent.

"I know you have a rule about not asking a client out. But what if the client wants to date you?"

Bryan grinned. "Well, maybe that might be different. But I don't want to get you in trouble."

"You won't. Mrs. Weston isn't in charge anymore. Wade is and you know how he and Maddie met."

"You make an excellent case. But are you sure?" Bryan looked a little hesitant and Melanie sensed that he was worried that she might change her mind.

"I've never been so sure," she said.

"Well then, I think I need another good night kiss."

CHAPTER 11

*M*elanie had a lazy Sunday. She slept in, did laundry and then met her sister Melissa and Jack for a delicious roast beef dinner at their house. After they ate, Jack collapsed in the living room to watch football and the two sisters decided to go for a walk. They ate early at a little past two so it was more like a late lunch and the sun was shining even though it was chilly. But it wasn't windy or snowing so they both agreed that it was ideal weather for a walk around the neighborhood.

"So, tell me all about last night. Did you have fun? Were there any sparks? Who else did you see there?"

Melanie filled her in on everything, including the end of the evening and the very special good night kiss. Melissa stopped when she heard the news and stared at her sister.

"He's the one, isn't he? Jaclyn was right. She's always right. Or rather, the fairies are. But what do you think?"

Melanie grinned. "I think he really might be the one for me. I've never felt this way about anyone. So comfortable with him yet really attracted too. I think about him all the time and look forward to seeing him."

"You've got it bad." Melissa laughed. "That's how it was with Jack too, only he was the one that realized it first. It took me a while to catch up. I just knew I really liked being around him."

"I think I knew first. Bryan's been the hesitant one. But he also got dumped not too long ago and I think has been feeling low about that."

"Afraid of being rejected again," Melissa said. "That makes sense."

"And he has that silly rule about not dating a client." Melanie grinned. "I pointed out to him that it would be different if the client wanted to date him."

Melissa laughed. "You actually said that?"

"I did! And then I kissed him. And I think he liked it."

"Good! I'm really happy for you."

"Thanks. Enough about me. Let's talk about you. How is your book doing?"

"Surprisingly well! My print copies arrived yesterday so they'll be going in the store on Monday and my ebook sales are much better than I thought they would be at this point. I have ten reviews already! And I don't even know these people. So it's complete strangers reading my book."

"Wow. I'm not at all surprised though that it's doing well. Are you working on another one?"

"Yes, and I'm almost done with it. I should finish it by the end of the week and then off it goes to the editor."

"That's so fast. It took you a lot longer with the first one, didn't it?"

"It did. But now I know what I'm doing and I have myself on a schedule. I get up an hour earlier than I used to and I write every morning for three hours before I go into the store. It's just the right amount of time and I do it every day, so the words add up fast."

"That's great! I look forward to reading this one too." It started to snow suddenly, so they decided to head back. And as glad as Melanie was to be driving a car that was good in snow, she still wasn't eager to go far.

"I'm going to head home, in case this decides to turn into something."

❄

*M*elanie went into work early Monday morning. Mondays were always busy at the gym. She was in a good mood and looking forward to seeing Bryan after work at the food pantry. She hadn't heard from him on Sunday but didn't really expect to as he'd told her he'd see her on Monday. Still she found herself wondering what he was up to. Her sister was right. She had it bad. She was too busy to think about much of anything though as she had training sessions all morning and then her weekly meeting with Wade in the afternoon.

She finally had a break at noon and was just about to eat the salad she'd brought for lunch when Natalie called to let her know she had a delivery at the front desk. She wasn't expecting anything so was curious as she walked out front. She stopped short when she saw the gorgeous flower arrangement on the counter.

"Those are for me?" She looked at Natalie in confusion. Surely they were for someone else.

Natalie nodded. "It's your name on the envelope. They just came from the new floral shop that opened up. Pushing Daisies."

"Oh. Melissa mentioned that was going to be opening soon. It's just a few doors down from the gift shop." She stepped closer to take a closer look.

They had done a beautiful job. The square cut glass vase held an explosion of roses—vivid pinks, reds and delicate white sprays of baby's breath. She checked the name on the card to make sure it was really for her, and apparently it was. She pulled the small card out of the envelope and smiled as she read it. "Thinking of you. Hoping your night was as wonderful as mine was. Happy Monday. Bryan."

"They're really lovely," Natalie said.

"They are, aren't they?" Melanie agreed as she picked up the arrangement and brought it into her office. She set it on the corner of her desk. It made her room smell fantastic. She called Bryan to thank him and got his voice message. She knew he was busy so she left a quick message thanking him and said she'd see him later. For the rest of the afternoon, every time she looked up and saw his flowers, she smiled.

Wade tapped on her door which she'd left ajar, at a few minutes past two.

"Come on in," she said.

He came in and settled in the chair across from her desk. He sniffed the air and looked around until he saw the flowers.

"Smells good in here. I see you have an admirer."

"Bryan sent them. I guess that means we're dating. I hope that won't be a problem?" Melanie decided to just put it out there so there hopefully wouldn't be any issues.

Wade laughed. "Why would there be? Bryan's a great guy. I approve....not that you need my approval!"

"So, there's no rule about not dating clients?"

Wade sighed. "I know that's what my mother would like. I struggled with it before I started dating Maddie. Especially now that we are in charge, I don't plan to enforce that particular rule. I'd have to apply it to myself to be fair, and I have no intention of getting a divorce!"

Melanie laughed. "I was hoping you'd say something like that. How is Maddie feeling by the way?"

Wade's light-hearted tone changed. "She's not good actually. We ended up at the ER yesterday and they've put her on total bed rest for the next few months. They consider this a high-risk pregnancy now."

"Oh, I'm sorry to hear that."

"We'll manage, but she won't be back to work for a while. A long while. Fortunately we are well staffed in the spa now and have people who can step up and cover for her."

"That's good."

"So, I don't think we have a whole lot to discuss today. Everything seems to be going well. I saw that we picked up a bunch of new reviews, all four and five stars on the MyTown site."

"We did. We had a good response to the email I sent out asking people to please help by leaving a review. We still have those really negative ones. I think I know who may be behind it." She told Wade her theory about Amy and the fact that her fiancé, Troy, ran the biggest health club in town.

Wade frowned. "It's not my intention to harm any other businesses. I see Idaho Fitness catering to a very different audience, the low monthly fee, no frills, bargain shoppers. We're more expensive but offer more amenities."

"That's how I see it too. I have an idea, that may or may not work, but I wanted to run it by you first." Melanie shared her thoughts with Wade and waited for his feedback.

"Go ahead and give it a try. It's worth a shot. As you said, we're different markets so if we can help rather than hurt our competitors, I'd rather do that."

"I was hoping you'd say that."

Melanie had noticed that Amy's trial month was up on Thursday and that she had a session booked with Melanie. She had no idea if her crazy idea would work, but was curious to see if it might help.

CHAPTER 12

elanie left the gym at three thirty to get to the food pantry by a quarter to four. They were to start handing out the turkeys and bags of food at four. Jess was there when she arrived and Bryan and Cameron arrived a few minutes later. There were a few other volunteers there too that Melanie didn't know, along with a few youth who helped bring out the boxes of refrigerated items, the blocks of cheese, butter and cans of whipped cream they would add to each bag that went out. They also set up a table of assorted pies so each family could choose which flavor they wanted to add to their bag.

Bryan walked over to say hello while Cameron stopped to chat for a minute with Jess.

"Hope your week is getting off to a good start?" He asked as he reached her.

"A wonderful start. Thank you so much for the flowers, they're beautiful!" She went to give him a hug, but he found her lips instead and gave her a warm welcome kiss that took her by surprise."

"Oh. That was nice!"

"I thought so," Bryan said with a grin. "I'm glad you liked the flowers. I think I have to head outside for turkey duty now." He wandered off while Cameron came her way and explained that Jess wanted the two of them to check people in as they came to pick up their food.

"They'll check in with us, then pick out their pies and head outside to get their turkeys on the way to their cars."

They spent the next two hours checking in a steady line of people. When they were almost done, there was a brief lull and they finally had a chance to chat a little.

"I was so sorry to miss the event the other night. My parents said they had a great time and I know Bryan did. I haven't seen him look this happy in a long time." She smiled but then looked more serious as she said, "He's really special to me and he was really hurt when Amy ended things. I don't want to see him go through that again."

Melanie nodded. "I think he's really special too."

Cameron relaxed a little. "Yeah, I think you do. My parents liked you a lot too, by the way. I thought that was a good sign. They never really warmed up to Amy."

They got busy again as the last few families of the day came in at once.

When they finished, Melanie went out for burgers with Bryan and they chatted for hours about anything and everything. They never seemed to run out of things to talk about. The next day they went through the same routine and when they gave out the last Christmas bag and turkey, they cleaned up and then everyone went to the Mexican restaurant on Main Street that Bryan had mentioned. Jake met them there and Wade too. He'd come earlier to help give out turkeys with Bryan.

They ordered margaritas and several platters of nachos and chicken wings.

"Maddie was sorry that she couldn't be here with everyone," Wade said as he raised his margarita. "But I told her we'd raise a glass in her honor. To Maddie."

"To Maddie," everyone said. Melanie took a sip of her drink. Margaritas always made her think of being on vacation and she couldn't imagine anything else going better with Mexican food.

"I feel so fortunate," she said to Bryan softly.

"What do you mean?" he asked.

"I have so much. A job I love, and my sister and I both have trust funds. Our parents left us well off when they died unexpectedly. I'd gladly give it all back to have more time with them though. I guess I'm just feeling emotional, being the time of year and all. And seeing all these people who are struggling, who are having a run of really bad luck. I guess I maybe feel a little guilty or something."

Bryan took her hand and squeezed it. "You have nothing to feel guilty about. You are lucky, but you're also doing something to help. That's all that matters."

She smiled. "I hope so."

After they finished their drinks and food, Bryan and Melanie walked out together and stood by Melanie's car for a while, chatting and occasionally kissing, while Bryan had his arms around her to keep her warm. Finally the cold got to them and Melanie shivered so hard that Bryan laughed.

"We should probably head home. I'll call you tomorrow."

*B*ryan hummed to himself as he pulled up to Jaclyn's house the next day around eleven. Her kitchen hutch and shelves that he'd built were ready to be installed. Jaclyn heard his truck coming and had the door open for him. He carried everything in and secured it all in place.

"What do you think?" He asked once everything was positioned the way he wanted it.

Jaclyn clapped her hands together with delight, startling two rabbits that were dozing by the heater vent in the corner.

"It's simply beautiful. Perfect. Just what I imagined. You are a magician!"

"I'm glad you like it."

Jaclyn handed him a check written in her shaky, delicate handwriting.

"Check the amount, make sure it's enough," she instructed him.

He glanced at the check. It was the exact amount on the invoice.

"It's perfect, thanks." He stuck the check in his pocket and turned to leave, but Jaclyn wasn't done with him yet.

"Stay for a cup of tea? I just took a fresh batch of cookies out of the oven. I'm curious to see if you like this combination as much as Melanie did. I took some into the gym recently."

Bryan grinned. "You don't have to ask me twice."

"Have a seat then. Get comfortable."

He did as instructed while Jaclyn fussed about the kitchen, pouring hot water for tea from a steaming kettle and setting a plate of cookies in the middle of the table. She brought two cups of tea over and gave one to Bryan and sat down to enjoy the other one herself.

"Go ahead, try one. These are snickerdoodle with raspberry. I think I like them almost as much as plain snickerdoodle. That's what I'm famous for you know."

"I've heard." Bryan bit into a cookie and gave Jaclyn a big thumbs up.

"This is a winner."

"Good. Now that we've got that out of the way I have another question for you. When are you and Melanie going to get engaged? Times a wastin' you know."

Bryan almost choked on his cookie. "What do you mean? We just started dating."

Jaclyn shook her head. "And that took you long enough, didn't it? What are you waiting for? You're both crazy about each other. Why not get married and get going with the rest of your life?"

"I've never really been one to rush into things," Bryan explained.

"And how has that worked out for you?"

Bryan laughed. She did have a point there.

"It took you a long time to figure out that Amy wasn't the one for you. Did you ever feel about her the way you feel about Melanie?"

That was an easy question. "No. That was very

different." Bryan was unsure of his feelings for Amy for a long time and they were always conflicted. He wanted to feel about her the way that he felt about Melanie, but he'd never felt this way about anyone before. So, he'd thought that with Amy maybe that was as good as it would ever get.

"So, you see what I'm saying then." Jaclyn smiled and reached for another cookie. "I'm glad we had this conversation."

"Me too."

When Bryan left Jaclyn's house, instead of taking a right and heading back to the office, he turned left towards Main Street. There was another stop he wanted to make.

*M*elanie met Amy for what she guessed would be her final session Thursday afternoon.

"This really is a nice club," Amy said as Melanie showed her a new piece of equipment that had just come in.

"It's important to Wade, the owner, that members have a really good experience. If you ever have any suggestions or feedback that could help us do better, we'd welcome it. There's a suggestion box at the reception desk and Wade is excited to give a generous gift certificate for any suggestion that we use."

"That's a great idea." Amy sounded impressed.

"We surveyed out members a few months ago and asked them what was most important to them and what we weren't currently offering that they really wanted and then we gave it to them."

"What was it?" Amy sounded curious.

"Expanded childcare. Having the hours start a little earlier and go a little later opened up a bigger window for when mothers would be able to use the club and it made the difference for some in which club they decided to go to. That's how important the issue was for them."

"Oh, that's really interesting."

"I know some of them are on tighter budgets and probably would go to the other big gym in town, Idaho Fitness I think it's called? Their monthly fees are lower but their hours aren't as good for childcare. That's just a quick example."

"That makes sense."

"Wade doesn't feel like we really compete with them though. Because we serve different markets. We always mention them for instance if someone calls for information and say that they can't afford to come here."

"You do?" Amy sounded surprised. "That's really nice."

Melanie nodded. "Wade believes that we're all part of the same community and what goes around comes around. I like to think that, but sometimes I'm not so sure, given what's been happening lately." She noticed a range of emotions flash across Amy's face and wondered if what she was saying was sinking in at all.

"What's been happening?" Yes, she had her on the hook, now to reel her in.

Melanie leaned in and spoke softly as if she was sharing a secret, "I probably shouldn't say anything, but I've been a little worried for Wade as we've had a flurry of really nasty reviews. I don't think he's seen them yet and I'm just hoping that maybe they might disappear before he does. Because they're just so unfair, the things that they say."

"Oh. Yeah, bad reviews are awful. I wouldn't want him to see them either." Amy looked uncomfortable at the thought. Melanie crossed her fingers and hoped that maybe those reviews might go away soon.

"Well, enough about that. What else shall we work on? How about some free weights?"

CHAPTER 13

The next two weeks were a whirlwind. Melanie saw Bryan almost every day and on the days they didn't see each other, they always talked on the phone. They hunkered down during another blizzard that was even worse than the one before, but this time it didn't take them by surprise. Melanie was glad to see that her Outback really was good in the snow. She drove to Bryan's house and then to the grocery store before the snow came down too hard. They stocked up on all kinds of snacks and had a movie marathon with big bowls of buttered popcorn, and the cats curled up beside them.

The week before Christmas they had so much fun participating in almost all of the holiday activities going on at the ranch. Melanie cheered Bryan on as he tried his hand at the snowmobile races and he was happy that he didn't come in dead last and beat his time from last year. The weather on Christmas Eve was cold but clear and calm, perfect for the ornament hanging ceremony on the ranch. They attended the Christmas Eve service at the church, which was always one of Melanie's favorite services. As they exited the church and walked outside, it was starting to snow ever so slightly and it was a magical sight to see.

Bryan took her hand as he walked her home to her cabin. His truck was parked right outside.

"Before I go home, I have a little something I want to give you, for your tree."

"You got me an ornament?" Melanie was touched. She had shared with Bryan that she collected Christmas ornaments and every year added a special new one to her collection.

"I did. I'll just get it out of the truck." He stopped and got a small gift bag out of his truck before they went inside. "This isn't all I got you. I have something else. I figured I'd see you tomorrow for dinner at my parents' and we'd exchange our gifts then. This is just something to open tonight." He handed her the bag and waited for her to look inside.

"Okay." She reached into the small bag and drew out a somewhat heavy cardboard box about the size of a baseball. She lifted the lid and gasped as she drew out the delicate ornament inside. It was a beautiful jeweled and hand painted egg that opened. She undid the clasp and swung the door open. The inside was just as beautifully painted but what took her breath away was what sat at the bottom of the egg. A vintage diamond engagement ring. She looked at Bryan with a mix of confusion, hope and joy.

He smiled and got down on one knee.

"These past few weeks have been the happiest of my life. The only thing that would make me happier would be to know that will never change. I love you, Melanie. Will you marry me?"

Melanie didn't hesitate for a second. "Of course I will!" She set the ornament down and pulled Bryan to his feet. "I love you too. So much!"

He kissed her soundly and then slid the ring onto her finger. She hung the ornament on her small tree while they discussed when they should get married.

"Do you want a big wedding?" Bryan asked nervously.

"Not particularly. Do you?"

He seemed relieved by her answer. "No! A big wedding takes time to plan and couldn't happen for longer than I'd like. I'd marry you tomorrow if you were willing."

Melanie laughed. She didn't want to wait either. "How about in a week? Melissa can stand up for me and we can go down to town hall, if that works for you. We can have a big party at your house after."

"That most definitely works for me!"

"Merry Christmas, Bryan," she said softly.

"Merry Christmas my soon-to-be wife."

EPILOGUE

New Year's Day

"That was the best New Year's Eve ever," Melanie said as Bryan handed her a mug of hot coffee. They were sitting at his kitchen table which was now their table. They'd gotten married the Friday before New Year's Eve at town hall and had everyone over that Sunday for a combined wedding reception and New Year's Eve party. Everyone had a great time and they were very happy to sleep in the next day. They didn't have to be anywhere and could just relax at home.

Melanie flipped through the newspaper while her new best friend, Rudy, slept by her feet. Bryan made breakfast for both of them and while they ate, she thought of something she'd forgotten to tell him.

"My little Jedi mind trick with Amy worked." She'd filled him in on their conversation.

"She took down the bad reviews?"

"Well, I still can't say for certain that it was her, but they are all gone now."

Bryan looked impressed. "Well done!"

"Thanks. Oh, and Wade says that Maddie is doing much better. She might be able to come off bed rest sometime next week. She still needs to take it easy though. She won't be able to go back to work still until after the baby comes."

"Oh, that's good. Her work is really physical."

"She's so good though. I'm not sure who I'll see while she's gone."

Bryan smiled. "I could give it a try."

Melanie laughed. "I won't say no to that." Her eyes fell on a new painting in the living room.

"I still can't believe you managed to get that painting for me. When they didn't call me, I thought it was gone."

He grinned. "I know. I happened to check for you before we left and saw that you'd been outbid and a few other people made bids too. So I added my bid and didn't want to get your hopes up, and then I thought it would make a good Christmas gift."

"It was perfect."

"Well, your gift wasn't too shabby either. I can't believe you noticed how interested I was in that trip." Melanie's gift to Bryan had been a long weekend trip to Boston and tickets to see a Red Sox game.

"You kept walking by it and staring at the history book about the Red Sox. Plus I figured it would be a good way to show you my city and take you to the North End for the world's best cannoli."

"One of my college roommates was from Boston. He used to talk about the Red Sox all the time. I've always wanted to go sometime. Your city is obsessed with sports!"

Melanie laughed. "Yes, that is very true."

"And a few months after opening day, we'll be moving into our new house," Bryan said.

Melanie was excited that Bryan had come up with a design that they both loved and it wouldn't just be her house, it would be theirs.

"I can't wait," she said.

She cleared their plates and put them in the dishwasher then topped off both of their mugs with a splash more coffee. Before she sat down, Bryan pulled her into his lap and kissed her.

"What was that for?"

"Do I need a reason to kiss my wife?" He asked and kissed her again.

"No, you don't. And I don't think I've mentioned yet today that I love you, have I?"

"I don't believe you have."

"Well, I do. And I always will."

Melanie saw Bryan's dimple flash as he grinned. "I love you too."

And then he kissed her.

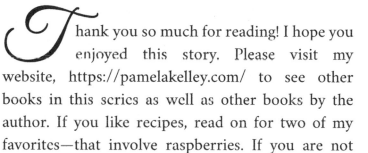

Thank you so much for reading! I hope you enjoyed this story. Please visit my website, https://pamelakelley.com/ to see other books in this series as well as other books by the author. If you like recipes, read on for two of my favorites—that involve raspberries. If you are not already on my mailing list, and would like to be notified about new releases or special sales and fun giveaways, please join my list.

If you are on Facebook, please join my Pamela Kelley reader group. It's a friendly group and I often share news and other updates there first as well as do exclusive giveaways around new releases. We also talk about books, food, pets and movies a lot. =)

AUTHOR'S NOTE

What you've read here about the Riston food pantry is based on my own experience as a volunteer with the food pantry at my church. It really does take a village. We have a team of volunteers and the pantry is funded by local donations. Most of our food comes from The Boston Food Bank and local companies like Panera and area restaurants.

The only difference is our big Turkey giveaway is for Thanksgiving instead of Christmas. If you are looking for a way to help in your area, most pantries are always grateful for additional volunteers, to help on delivery day, or to work a shift handing out food, or if you wanted to donate food, almost all dry goods are always welcome—especially staples like peanut butter, pasta, tuna, and canned items.

Raspberry Snickerdoodle Thumbprint Cookies

1 cup butter
    1 1/2 cups sugar
    2 large eggs
    2 3/4 cups flour
    2 teaspoons cream of tartar
    1 teaspoon baking soda
    1/4 teaspoon salt
    3 tablespoons sugar
    1 tablespoon cinnamon
    1 teaspoon vanilla
    Raspberry jam

Preheat oven to 350.
    Mix butter, sugar, vanilla and eggs in large bowl.

Combine flour, cream of tartar, baking soda and salt in another bowl. Add dry ingredients to butter mixture and mix well. Chill dough in refrigerator for 30 minutes. Mix sugar and cinnamon in a small bowl. Scoop dough into small balls, roll lightly in sugar mixture and place on ungreased cookie sheet. Press your thumb on top of cookie to make a small well and drop a half teaspoon or so of raspberry jam on each cookie. Bake for about ten minutes. Cool and enjoy!

Raspberry Overnight Oats

These are beyond delicious and so healthy, too.

1/2 cup Old Fashioned Oats
  1/2 cup Almond milk (or any milk)
  1 tablespoon Chia seeds (optional, adds protein)
  1 rounded teaspoon cocoa powder
  1 tsp maple syrup (I skip if using sweetened almond milk)
  1/2 cup raspberries (I use frozen)
  1 tablespoon natural peanut butter

Mix all ingredients except raspberries, then fold them in. Cover and refrigerate overnight. Enjoy your creamy oats for breakfast!

Made in United States
North Haven, CT
09 November 2021